PURE
SLUSH
BOOKS

LUST

7 Deadly Sins Vol. 1

Pure Slush Books
32 Meredith Street
Sefton Park SA 5083
Australia

Email: edpureslush@live.com.au
Website: https://pureslush.com/
Store: https://pureslush.com/store/

Original cover photograph copyright © Matthew Bowden
Cover design copyright © Matt Potter

ISBN: 978-1-925536-47-8

Also available as an eBook
ISBN: 978-1-925536-48-5

A note on differences in punctuation and spelling

Pure Slush Books proudly features writers from all over the English-speaking world.
Some speak and write English as their first language, while for others, it's their
second or third or even fourth language. Naturally, across all versions of English,
there are differences in punctuation and spelling, and even in meaning. These
differences are reflected in the work *Pure Slush Books* publishes, and accounts for any
differences in punctuation, spelling and meaning found within these pages.

Pure Slush Books is a member of the
Bequem Publishing collective
http://www.bequempublishing.com/

• MaKayla ALLEN • Paul BECKMAN • Robert BEVERIDGE • Rick BLUM • Corwin Grace BRAND • Ron CAMPBELL • Robert CARLTON • Steven CARR • Guilie CASTILLO ORIARD • Yuang CHANGMING • Carl CHAPMAN • Jan CHRONISTER • Linda M. CRATE • Judah Eli CRICELLI • Albert DeGENOVA • Andrea DIEDE • William DORESKI • Michael ESTABROOK • Sarah ETLINGER • Nod GHOSH • Ken GOSSE • Jack GRANATH • Andrew GRENFELL • John GREY • Shane GUTHRIE • Kyle HEMMINGS • Mark HUDSON • Robert IULO • Abha IYENGAR • Charles JACOBSON • Joanne JAGODA • Christine JOHNSON • Jemshed KHAN • Edith KNIGHT • Len KUNTZ • John LAMBREMONT Sr. • Ron LAVALETTE • Larry LEFKOWITZ • DS LEVY • Paul LEWALLAN • Peter LINGARD • JP LUNDSTROM • Jenean McBREARTY • Janet McCANN • Corey MESLER • T.C. MILL • David MILLER • Piet NIEUWLAND • Edward O'DWYER • Carl 'Papa' PALMER • M PAUSEMAN • Joseph S. PETE • Stephen V. RAMEY • Alex ROBERTSON • Ruth Sabath ROSENTHAL • Shawn Aveningo SANDERS • Jeff SANTOSUOSSO • Wayne SCHEER • Joseph SZEWCZYK • Angelina TAYLOR • Lucy TYRRELL • James WADE • Kenneth WAGNER • Rob WALKER • Alan WALOWITZ • Michael WEBB • Jeffrey WEISMAN • Robb T. WHITE • Nan WIGINGTON • Jeffrey ZABLE •

Contents

Poetry

Poetry

Bruise

Judah Eli Cricelli

Your words are foaming over
And your car is far away
But I'm a
Little major,
In the way,
Sincere
Endearing
Hard of hearing
Metallic mother
Metal earring
Eyes that watch me from the ceiling
All the lust that
Keeps me feeling
Scattered feels and
Scattered-feeling,
Down the wheels, along the road are
Magic markers,
Then you slowed now
Sticky-tape frown:
Tape it down
The skin that weeps
And shins that frown,
No sweat, though
Right?

You're just my light, you
Flicker when it's
Dark at night,
I'll draw for you in texta,
Right,
I might I
Might
And how I'd like to
Fight or flight the
Feelings that are shite
You're right:
The morning's kinda shitty
But I'm otherwise alright—
We're tight—
And by the way
I want to say
I'm feeling mostly fine today
If I could boast it
Half as close
Or be the ghost of
Burnt-up toast
Or feel some feeling in my toes
Or open doors when doors are closed

Or sneak a mouthful full of sand
Or bash my skull against my hand
Or rest my head against the wall
And bruise some bricks before they fall
I swear to God
I won't decay
I'll never let you fade away
'Cause everything is grey
And I won't
Lose this little lantern
That's been lighting up the way.

Affair

Jemshed Khan

Though we ward off our infidelities
with *Thou Shalt Not* and vows of chastity,
lust and wine still tilt our sauntering eyes
into sidelong glance and wicked candy:
My blood bangs out a bulge of rude desire.
Your finger sparkle slips from sight and care.
The cock-god struts and mounts the cuckold fire.
We are shakra; semen, sweat and pyre. Later,
we slip our selves back to separate homes.
You ninja-step your creaky hallway floors,
and I slow tiptoe into bedroom gloam.
You hear the sleepy puff and tug of snores.
An indelicate task still lies ahead:
To slithe unnoticed into married bed.

Lust Never Sleeps
(an acrostic)

John Lambremont Sr.

Longing beginning in one's early years;
Understand later it won't disappear;
Sexual organ that grows in one's head;
Trying desire for someone to bed.

None can control it, and few can suppress;
External forces cause internal stress;
Various manifestations, one theme;
Even will follow one into one's dreams, but
Reality isn't quite what one sees.

Seems like advancing years would this abate:
Last thought before sleep, first thought when awake;
Exacerbated by media forms;
Even a new industry was thus born;
Perhaps pure wretchedness, perhaps a norm;
Suffer it silently, or write a poem.

My Lustful Woman, Who's Such a Wonder

Yuan Changming

Among evergreens of an unknown
Hill, can come tight on top of me
Like a patch of heaven, sagging herself
Down for Penetration, Pop Pop Pop!

Let me grow harder and taller
Wrapping me with her dripping mists
Stroking me with her inner tongues
Then I roll over her

Bloated shape, ready to rise
Again, and again
And drift with me in a cloud
After planting my selfhood into earth

As deeply as a tree
An everlasting erection

A Lust for Land

Lucy Tyrrell

I burn with lust, a lust for land,
embrace earth's skin, so smooth-caressed
or rough from glacier's gravely wear.

I press hard granite, warmed in sun,
recline on slanting slab of rock
along the arc of salt-wet cove.

I lie as shadow near the birch,
its leaning frame stark, winter-bare,
ache-yearning under rising moon.

I long to spoon in tender arms
of meadow grasses, drowsed by wings—
warm summer evening's fire-lamps.

I wait in darkness, rocky tors
jut-angling from the bedding planes,
desire red lips of mesa walls,
while milky stars spill miles of sky.

Diesel

Robert Beveridge

Nine geisha judge the proceedings,
the tangle of limbs and tongues shunned
by all but the hardiest of explorers. You stare
into blue eyes rimmed by kohl and firelight
as her beautiful freckled cheeks take you
in deeper than ever before. Your reward
the salty kiss afterwards, but for now
your tongue has other uses. Fingertips
bless every piece of you with abandon,
the very ground consecrated with excited
utterances. Someone pushes into you
from behind, delicious girth and sensation
of fullness. Teeth on each nipple. You cannot
hold out longer. And as her perfect lips
meet yours you wonder when this became
a trial, and whether you will be found worthy.

Dental Impressions

Shawn Aveningo Sanders

I.

Your toothbrush slid over on mine.
It started vibrating. And all I could think—
how dirty my teeth felt.
And I liked it.

II.

You were so hard last night—
I was afraid I might chip a tooth.

III.

I didn't come here looking for
gentle. Go ahead—
Put me under.
Drill deep.
Fill my cavity.

A Night Out with the Boys

John Grey

A summer night, walking downtown,
we're sweaty with light, with noise,
stopping at bar after bar,
like we're the hustlers we see,
the drunks that stumble over us,
the loose-tongued ones who've reached
the point where they can tell the world
about everything they feel.
A summer night, between their lives
and ours. No longer in our long,
contented marriages but not in their
ragged, vulgar, spewing, single lusts either.
We don't pretend we'll want the ones
we want forever. But we're not
quite at the point where our
longings last one night, where they're
spinning on a stool, showing leg,
half-breast, a swathe of dyed blonde hair.

A summer night, and try as our imaginations
might, the best will not be two hours
in sloppy sheets, grappling with strangers,
like happens to the ones we drink with.
Before the night is done, they'll reconnoiter,
chat up, fuzzy brain their way into a
Back Bay flat of temporary delights. But
for married guys and bar blow-flies alike,
the joy is what convinces us there
is no joy. Our drinking buddies won't
remember because they'll be blitzed out
of their skulls. We don't remember
because it won't stop happening.

The Reckoning

Alan Walowitz

Ever since the quarantine,
I take it in from this window:
the girls patrol the streets in packs.
At the up-all-night, the neon
slowly crawls: *Beer. Redemption. Snacks.*
all to the sound of a martial tattoo.
No sign of forgiveness here
where the streetlamps' light in sharp relief–
women-at-arms and guarding the night.

The law is clear and I stand warned.
Thou shall not stare or, gawk, or leer,
but, look, here's one who takes my breath
and what's a man to do–I don't dare
as in days of old, put a hand in my pants
while the other holds the blind half-closed.
Her breasts bob in her shirt–and I can barely breathe–
hips mold to denim as she moves dreamlike and slow
to let the others know I've been seen–
her hair, a soft pendulum,
counts down my time.

The firing squad beats down the door;
my prints all over the pane.
Mothers of daughters I've never imagined,
sisters I've never dreamed,
harass me with sharp epithets.
Bayonets poised, I'm forced to the courtyard,
but court is not convened.
Though I repent, and cop a plea,
they shoot, and in my unintended way,
improve man's capacity
for change.

Artifice

Rick Blum

When I first saw her
at the Christmas party,
she had meticulously molded herself
into a statuesque beauty:
hair sprayed into shocks
of NICE'N EASY blonde locks;
skin air-brushed, layer by layer,
to achieve a wrinkleless sheen;
eyes laded under smoky blue lids
with thick, long lashes;
lips lined and glossed rebel red
to mesmerize the fawning crowd
of lustful men gathered 'round
her apocryphal pedestal
near the cold shrimp and hot wings.

Weeks later I saw her
in the Whole Foods produce aisle,
me searching for broccolini,
she inspecting bags of baby carrots.
She looked only vaguely familiar,
someone my brain had on file
but had lost the key to unlock
that particular drawer. I was scanning
her universal mom-shopping garb –
yoga pants and zip-up hoodie –
for clues to her identity
when she looked back to see me staring.
She smiled (letting fluorescent rays
illuminate the baby crow's feet
framing her doe brown eyes),
brushed a wayward strand of hair
from her face and said,
Hi, Rick. How's it going?
The sound of her voice instantly brought
her former image into vivid relief,
and I realized, much to my surprise,
that she was better looking than she looked
when I first saw her at the Christmas party.

Elemental

Kenneth Wagner

If I am water
you better be earth
so I can sculpt your body
with shallow tributaries in the hollow
of your collarbones   with streams
turned rivers flowing over your
ribs and down in a fast sinuous fall
twisting in the crosscurrent
of your smooth ivory stomach
and when I reach the crease
in your hip I'll slow and ease
my way down to rivulet   for a while
until I cool and turn into the sharp cold
on your inner thigh
that wakes the elemental you
and reminds you that together
we are as ignitable as air and fire
and that the blaze of us
can out-summer the sun
but only if you are earth   damn it
and I am water

Lust

Janet McCann

Saints seem to have to wrestle
With lust most frequently, maybe
Because of their high energy. Francis
Threw himself into snowbanks to cool
His, and Augustine struggled with desire
So much that looking back in guilt still held
A glitter of remembered satisfaction. That energy:
Fierce inner force that attaches first
To the wrong thing, works itself out in sweaty
Pleasure, then starts up again. You don't hear
Of idle saints, sitting in pleasant hammocks
Reading the Bible, saintly dogs at their feet,
Or even baking pastries for the convent.
The Juggler of Our Lady nearly fainted
From exertion, but came to when She blessed him.
Even wrestling with one's laziness
Takes effort, though one would not call it lust.
Inertia, anomie. *Ich hatte Lust*, my German aunt
said, but she only meant, I just did it
because I felt like it.

A One-Time Star

Jeffrey Zable

I was a teenage movie star,
and when I wasn't on the set,
I was always in my trailer
with female fans
getting good head
or bouncing 'em up and down.

I hardly had energy
to sign any autographs
but my agent said
it was good for my career,
so I made myself do it
scrawling out a "J"
and following with a "Z."

My life was a dream
until the advent of color
which exposed all my pimples
and the gaps in my teeth.

Now here I am,
a two-bit hustler,
living off the bad graces of women
who are over the hill.

Dr(own) Me

Ron Campbell

Slander me with compliments.
Poison me with praise.
Slather love upon me
Like it was mayonnaise.

Batter me with flattery.
Obfuscate my self-regard.
Pester me with blessings.
Don't make me work too hard.

Give me a tearful earful.
Acclimate me to acclaim.
Throw out my self-doubt
With the bath water of your gaze.

Substantiate all my delusions,
Berate me with adulation,
Disparage me with a barrage
of sabotage.

Libel me with sweet nothings,
Gorge me with somethin' somethings,
Corroborate my best suspicions,
And in a sea of kisses, drown me.

Eating Grapefruits

Jeff Santosuosso

My older sister and her friends
taught me all about grapefruits.
How to choose them, how to slice them and prepare them,
how to eat them, and how to juice them.
The fingers and hands revealed all.
"Discolorations on the skin are ok,
you don't eat with your eyes.
Use your fingers to feel the fruit.
The skin will tell you about the flesh."
We practiced every week at the grocery store.

Then, home to slice them open, eat and drink. Hands again.
"Grasp firmly, but don't squeeze too hard.
Use both hands, cut like you mean it."
That scared me at first, but I trusted my hands,
mastered the feel.
Time to try the grapefruit knife:
"Slide the knife into the section and go around.
Can you feel the knife slide through it?
It should feel like an extension of your fingers."

Yes.
That knife described the insides.
Over and over, freeing all sections.
I had to learn to hold the outsides,
to grip them so that I could enjoy the insides.

"Now spoon it out."
The spoon took the knife's place, just as easily, too.
I scooped each section out, putting it to my lips,
over and over.
"Do you like it?"
Yes. They only had to ask me once, but they'd ask every time.
Sometimes I'd just smile and lick my lips and chin.

"Now squeeze out the juices. That's the best part!"
I grabbed the half, this time in my palm,
and squeezed with fingers, thumb, palm and wrist.
The juice cascaded, squirted, splashed right out!
That first time was a mess, but I learned to control the juices.
I'd squeeze them right into my mouth!
Yes, it would spray on my cheeks, my nose, my lips,
even my nose and chin, but it was worth it
To feel the wetness on my lips and tongue.

Do It Yourself

Ron Lavalette

A word to the wise:
it pays to clean your tool
when the job's finally done
even if you only dip it
in the old paintcan
once in a blue moon
or you're one of those
six-jobs-a-day
touch-up artists;
whether it's a straight,
long-bristled detail brush
with a customized grip
or a bulky twelve-inch
cement floor roller,
no matter what kind of
medium you're spreading
—matte, satin, or glossy —
you'll save yourself a big
headache later on if you
wash it down afterwards.

And you guys with the big
power sprayers: remember
to wipe down your hoses
and flush them out often.
You don't want them to
get all gummed-up and
rot away from inside;
and pay special attention
to that tricky nozzle area.

Always remember this:
a well-maintained tool will
give you years of service,
but if you don't scrub it
down between jobs
you'll pay for it in the end.

Original Sin

Jan Chronister

If menstruation is the curse
then menopause is redemption.
Having spent more than half our lives
bleeding, women are finally free
from cramping, pms-ing
counting days, watching dates.
The flow stops, faucets turn
the tap is off. Lust is fun again.

dogging

Rob Walker

dogs caught *in flagrante delicto* show self-consciousness,
ears back   faces like embarrassed chimps
twice as awkward as a humped dog defecating
on a pristine lawn

caught red-faced, red-handed, red knobbed
hormones doing the job
as the crime
blazes

Away

Albert DeGenova

Beware of falling in love with singers
I tell our son, it is
a tragic, genetic flaw. And I'm struck
once again – a woman's voice
like a goose down comforter folded and
quartered, alone on a single bed
beckoning from the car stereo
of a taxi in Frankfurt, Germany,
thousands of miles away from you –

Elke's Australian accent is
flooding this backseat with blue
eyes, when the cabby tells me
the singer is Eva, a Brit,
and I feel your
        wine-wet lust
on my fingertips,
your
        long low brown-haired voice
singing
    something

about the *Going Home Blues*,
and making the coffee
and the narcissus in bloom
in your garden in Chicago
and our roof that needs to be mended
and we will.

A Woman Dancing Alone

Edward O'Dwyer

An egg-yolk sun has set,
and a solitary woman is dancing in a bar.
It has a jukebox, but it isn't really
a dancing bar, and the few occasions
it might have been, you'd imagine,
led to some trouble. She's dancing with nobody

but, then again, she might say
she is dancing with herself,
leading herself, being led by herself.
More likely, she would say
she's dancing with everyone here,
especially the men, though
tonight's drinkers are nearly all men,
none dressed well, none clean-shaven,
tattoos spiralling up their arms.

All of their eyes are stealing glances
at her, planting thoughts on her
like kisses, the wet kind.
Their intentions caress her
gyrating contours, nestle inside
the measured crevices her choice
of outfit affords their leers.

She'll be the subject of more than
a few remarks that ladies, publicly,
wouldn't feel flattered by.
Privately is always another matter.
She'll not mind what's said, though.
To her, it's all currency, just like
the attentions of their eyes are, just like
their faces are, faces showing
thirsts that will not be sated
by any amount of beer or whiskey.

No one here cares about what dreams
she had once, or has never had.
No one is going to ask, although soon
someone is going to approach her,
believing, no doubt, it's high time
she met a real man.

That's where it's headed, this scene.
That's when things get interesting.
As if a man is ever what this woman
has wanted from life and, more to the point,
from here, from tonight, from dancing alone
at a bar that isn't a dancing bar, dancing
with herself, with no one, with everyone.

Goddess of All My Hours

Corwin Grace Brand

Wake up with wanton thoughts
about how you might be ready
to take me in
between your wet thighs
and hold me tightly
pressed, pinned, and throbbing
with a morning urge
that aches to find release
closer to your womb
than I've ever felt before.

Drift through the day with wanderlust
over how I need to see you smile
when it lights up my mind
like no other force
on earth can manage
with its power beyond the pale
to send me swooning
and looking to start a fire
that transcribes you signals of smoke
of this burning passion everlasting.

Lay my head down at night
to seek your soul in dreams
where hearts can meet
on the astral plane
that has no end or beginning
but pulses in the present moment
transcending the scope of time
as this love echoes in tune
with the rhythm of emotions
you have ignited to last forever.

Lust and the Life Cycle

Alex Robertson

To be sociable
   beyond one's family
Liking someone
Whether it be
Inner beauty or face value
Visitors at home
   or strangers in a public place
Provides a stance
Virtuous before corruption
Or realisation of the life cycle
Significant knowledge
Takes over the mind
In one's adolescence

Innocence gone
Once bodily workings are realised
Talks of birds and bees
Or Biology lessons
   start to sink in
A first kiss passionately given
Hugs against another
In a getting to know you fashion

Gentle interaction
As if feeling fruit
Gesticulations of peeled bananas
    or peaches richly sought after
Tender touching
Manipulating the flesh
Rather than biting the pomegranate
(Seed to be spilt
    at a later time)
Expectant growth of a gamete
With the intention of the act
To procreate
    For the love of another

Monty Python described it right
Sacred or not
    one's background reflects contraception
A divide between agape
    and the stiff upper lip
Still carries between churches
In a post-clerical world

Maturity versus feebleness
Where longing is passé
And no longer a consideration
In the senior years
Viagra considered in stable situations
Meat markets never visited
A feeling for affection AND company
As growing old together
Is a better option than a life alone
Company in retirement village
Or fraternity in a unit block
Managing the esprit de corps
Rather than the full dance card
Nightclubs are for the nippers now…
And contact (real or virtual)
Happens with being the IT girl or boy

Lust like youth
    fades
But amity endures a lifetime

Evening wind cools

Piet Nieuwland

The sky ablaze with the galactic bulge
And high-flying dream-liners
Make their way to the land of the rising sun
A hot moon dissolves into black
Wind that races brilliant across the plains
Night rains and the scent of spindled cedars
Sleep in the solitudes of your eyes
On this green island where we met
The sound of the sea on Opunake beach
Curves with black magnetics and infinities
Beneath Taranaki, the primal image
A shrine capped in shields of snow gleam
And the lust in your Beethoven piano sonatas
Your pale green dress scorched by lightning
Coral flowers of turquoise and wet red

blood lust

Linda M. Crate

i know this blood lust is wrong, but i want to spill all of yours;
let it hit the cobbled street and watch as it makes a red river
beneath a blood red moon—i want you to know the banshee
cry of my deepest anger and feel my harpy's claws, i want you
to know the dark side of my moons; because i gave you nothing
but my deepest truths and all the love of my heart and it wasn't
enough to fulfill the coffers of your greed—so i want to spill out
all your nightmares so i can slaughter them with all of my light
because i am the keeper of golden moons, and i gave myself
away to you for a price that wasn't even half my worth; but the
truth is you never could have afforded me should have kept my
distance and my heart—i was wrong, but i won't regret loving
you; because even if you didn't love me i can be honest and say
i really did care; once upon a time when i didn't know you were
a silver-toothed devil—but i know that karma will hit you
harder than i ever could so i'll let her, and i will look down on
you upon the ground when you beg me for help; i'll let
someone else reach down and lift you up before i walk away—
just so you can see that your lust isn't something that destroyed
me nor will my love for you be strong enough to make me turn
around and accept you back in my life not even as a friend.

Suzi the Stripper

Mark Hudson

Suzi was a good girl who just couldn't get her
act straight. Her parents died when she was a teen in
a car accident, and she was forced to work at a grocery
store to pay rent on her apartment, eventually dropping
out of high school.

So when she really needed money bad, she went
to where all the pretty girls went when they really wanted
good money, the local strip club. There were great tips,
and you really had to be good-looking, able to dance
on a pole, and deal with horny men.

She'd been doing it for about six months, and
she had to admit, she was making better money than
the grocery store. She was making really good money.

One night, the house was packed. Not an empty
seat. Suzi was doing her pole dance, and the men were
loving it. She was butt naked, and she had a killer body.

When out of the audience, out of nowhere, a
man had stripped out of his clothes because he got too
aroused. He was a four foot man with a fifteen inch
penis.

He raced up on stage, erection leading him on.
When Suzi saw him coming, she made it part of the act.
He began to make love to her furiously, sticking it right
in and pounding in and out, to the cheers of the crowd.

He came abruptly, inside of her and some dribbling
on the stage. Then he got his clothes, it was a green
leprechaun suit, and he raced out the alley exit,
pulling up his pants as he ran away.

Well, a little later, Suzi found out she was
pregnant, and could no longer work as a stripper.
But she had gone down in the history of the strip club
as "the most exciting act" they ever had.

She became a single mom on food stamps,
and disability. But the moment she gave birth
to her baby, she could tell that it was going
to be a "disturbed little lad."

Whoever the mystery "leprechaun" was,
his bastard son seemed to be a "chip off the
old block."

I would tell you about this little
troublemaker, but that would be a completely
different story.

Suzi had nothing but grief from her son.
Is there any happy ending to this story? Well,
you can make one up if you want to. It seems
like love is better than lust. But usually lust
is often a stronger driving force than love.
But hopefully there is hope for all
of us losers down on Earth, the Suzis
of the world, and the mad leprechauns
racing through the world, their
asses to the wind
as they race from one debauchee to another.

Your Leather Outlook

William Doreski

Your motorcycle days are past,
at least for this year of sighs.
Autumn crackles in the streets
where the gunfire has abated
and cartoon characters settle
at outdoor cafes and autograph
their ghost-written memoirs in blood.

Stanzas of leaf and flower decay
in suburbs you've learned to avoid
because the cops know your Harley
and object to its loud exhaust.
You claim the noise is political,
protected speech, but no one agrees,
not even your mechanic, whose face
is a most pugnacious fist.

All summer you rattled the streets
of this preening city, blue smoke
bleeding into basement flats
to choke the low-rent infants
mewling in second-hand cribs.
Black leather nights prepared you
for the Orphic moment when
you'd look back and condemn me
to the bowels of Hades. Not guilty

of lusting for your favors
or admiring the portrait Jamie
Wyeth painted of you sprawled
on your slick and grinning machine.
But when I asked to ride behind you,
clinging as you tilted on curves,
you gaped in such frank disdain
that I more or less died on my feet.

The season's over, the early dark
has settled like a brood hen.
Maybe after a long slack winter
I'll rebirth myself and return
from the Hades of my night-sweats.
And maybe by then your leather
outlook will relent enough
to allow me to ride behind you
downtown to the harbor where
the stink of exhaust will dissipate,
leaving us friendly again.

Silence like the grave

MaKayla Allen

We fuck in the
library of the upper-class home
with the two cats
he's "cat-sitting" this weekend.

I lie back spread over an
ottoman reading book bindings
while he foams at the mouth
into me,
making sounds like
he is attempting to swallow
waves as they hit the sand
in wet explosions:

The owners have a lot of books on wood-working.

I don't orgasm.

When he sits
in the wing-back arm-chair
I put his hands on
the off-blue fabric
and hold his shoulders
avoiding looking directly:

he creaks like collected
furniture, comes like
a rocking chair
strained too far forwards.

I imagine his sperm like erected graves
embedded in my system, and
I read the bindings unmoving,
like collected furnishings at rest.

Like low-tide when there are no waves
to rock the surface.

Now Dina – the daughter of Leah, whom she had borne to Jacob – went out to look over the daughters of the land

Joanne Jagoda

Ema (Mama) let me go out,
    to share gossip with the local girls
    and see how they fashion their braids.
    I must get away from my brothers,
    who torment me from first light.

Daughter, your father, the Great One,
    would not approve
    of you walking alone
    without your brothers for escort
    while they tend cattle in the fields.

Ema, Ema I'm a good girl and old enough
    to enjoy a moment alone.
    and surely the God of heavens and earth
    will watch over me as I journey.

Dina, my daughter, your will
        is as mighty as the great cedars.
        Promise me you'll return
        before the skies meld violet.

Dear *Ema*, thank you, thank you,
        I'll not be late.
        I promise.

You there, pretty one… tarry a moment,
        you move as graceful as the doe.
        Turn about and
        let me gaze upon you.

You address **me**, Sir?
        Who is this handsome buck
        with brazen tongue and burning eyes?
        You're perhaps acquainted with my brothers?
        We are of the proud family of Jacob!

Oh most assuredly…
        we welcomed your Father, the Great One,
        to our land most graciously,
        and I bow humbly in the countenance of your
        loveliness.
        I am Shechem, son of Hamor the Prince.

I'll have her now…my loins swell
> *then her father will surely grant me*
> *her hand in marriage*
> *at a much reduced bride's price.*

Come, my pretty one
> yes, closer… be not afraid.
> Follow me down to the willows where it's shady;
> have a cool drink from my pouch,
> and rest upon the woven mats

Sir, I dare not be alone with you.
> *What will Ema and Abba (father) say*
> *but I do thirst in this heat of midday.*
> *What could be so wrong with a little sip?*
> One drink yes…then I'll be on my way.
> I seek your sisters.

Of course my pretty one. I'll take you
> to frolic with them in the meadows—
> *when I'm done with you.*

Ema, Abba, where are you?
> *Brothers hear my cries, help me…*

Jacob, revered husband
>my daughter has not returned by violet-dusk.
>I fear a wild beast has overtaken her.
>Tell me at once what you know.
>Your face is eclipsed with rage.

Wife, indeed a wild beast is to blame
>the son of Hamor
>found her on the road,
>and defiled her.
>She brings dishonor upon my house.
>Hah... your daughter is like you, an unruly spirit.
>I spit on you both.

Your words are pitiless... you pious fool,
>and they rip my heart asunder.
>Our girl is guilty only of being stubborn.
>She is just like **you...** her father.
>Reproach not your blameless child,
>instead punish the animal who violated her.

Yonder my sons come sporting from the field.
>When they hear what has befallen their sister
>their high spirits will ignite into fiery rage.
>They will avenge her honor
>and bring... **our** child home.

Oh husband, I fear the consequences
>of their unbridled anger...
>mothers will weep tomorrow.

The Ballad of His Love

Corey Mesler

He took his love out to the
street and walked it around
as if it would follow him
anywhere. It was an old
trick and a few people bought
it and their hearts expanded
and they began sending him
food and messages. Back at
home he kept his love in an
old locker, with his cleats and
wiffle balls. Sometimes lovers
visited and he locked the locker
and they scratched each other
like cats, crying, as the blood
surfaced, yes, God, do it like
that, yes, do it with all your heart.

Where Lust
Eventually Led Me

Ruth Sabath Rosenthal

Riding past the Museum
of Natural History & seeing the steps
I first took toward infidelity —
how far I descended.

My lover is history, has been
for some thirty-odd years, yet,
I remember the nervous excitement
still — how unashamed

& unnaturally good I'd felt. How
beyond stupid, thinking I would scale
those highs unscathed — so sure
I was just stepping into

my husband's footprints —
impressions he made long before
I ever thought of venturing to make hurt go
by going the ways of wayward flesh —

before I knew what I know now:
the crawl space one could carve
in a marriage preserved
for the children's sake.

Mysterious Package

Shane Guthrie

I got a package today, hefty, about 13" long,
addressed to Tequila Jones.
One side of the box was damaged,
I knew I shouldn't but I looked inside.
What I found there shocked me, and then excited me.

Of course I had to get these precious items
to their rightful owner.
The address wasn't hard to find
it was just a few blocks away
Jones on the mailbox.

Several nights running I'd drive by with the damaged box
thinking I'd do it.
She kept odd hours
sometimes the lights wouldn't turn on till late
different cars in the driveway.

Not too surprising, given what I found in that box
I considered taping it up
Would that be more suspicious?

Finally, one night, in a cold sweat
after circling the block twice
I parked on the street, rehearsed my speech
nonchalant, apologetic, innocent.

When she came to the door
she was somehow exactly what I'd expected.
Curious, confident, flirtatious eyes
Clearly I'd interrupted… something.

"Um, this was delivered, I'm sure by accident—
To my house, I didn't open it,
I thought you'd want these toys, Tequila
Can I, can I call you Tequila?"

"Mmmm, I've been waiting for these, thank you, honey
They were supposed to be here days ago."
She took the box in her elegant hands.
"Oh," she added, "looks like someone's been peeking."
And she looked me full in the face.

Shame flooded me
"Uh, no, heh heh, no, it was like that when I got it—"
"Do you need to be punished?"
she interrupted, with a raised eyebrow,
"because I do that."
My heart raced.
"But you knew that, didn't you,
that's why you're here, isn't it?"

"What? No. I mean, not really, but… maybe? This is weird."
"Come in, relax, it's OK to want it" she said,
not bothering to see if I was following.
She laid the box on the table.
I stepped over the threshold and into a new world.
Next to my box were two others exactly the same.

Valentine in a Time of War

Jack Granath

It was a business trip.
We didn't sit together on the plane
or at the conference or in the restaurant,
but back in that welter of professional rooms
I watched her rise and smooth her skirt
and look at me and smooth her skirt
again,
and suddenly I was at her side
asking how had she liked the keynote address,
"Investing in a Time of War."
She said she was bored
and, pointing out one of a
dozen snickering bureaucrats, told me,
I went down on him for no goddamn reason.
I confessed that I had always liked the word *pussy*.
Why so solemn? she said. Let's have sex in public.
I agreed, but we couldn't find a place that was public enough.
I think she had in mind tourists and flashbulbs.
I offered to tell her my life story.
No sir, she said. Not unless you've got one finger in my butt.
I apologized in advance for any reckless semen stains.

She said, that's okay, it's nothing compared
to what I'm going to do to you.
I said, I mauled your secretary once, in the archives.
She said, me too, and we knew that we had been used.
I mentioned that *vagina* is from the Latin for "sheath."
Think about it long enough and you'll see stars.
She knew it for a bunch of jabber I made up on the spot
and said that when she blew the guy he took a call on his cell
and that his climax made her think of vectors.
She decided she had forgotten
everything she learned in high school.
What about him? I asked, in no way actually concerned.
He got paged at the crucial moment and was rendered joyless.
So you're into degradation?
Nice try, pal, she said. You're not peeing on me.
We discussed the word *cunt* and how it makes my mouth go dry
and the concept of Valentines.
But it's so mean, she argued, adding, I'm gonna
use your face like a fucking circus ride.
It was then I realized
I would never place my sex between her jaws.
All I really want is to touch your body the way you touched
your body when you got up out of that chair, I said.
She thought about it, surprised and oddly flattered,
and consented.
I passed my hand across the wonderful curve of her bottom,
and we flew back to Chicago.
At nine-thirty the next morning I saw her secretary
staggering down the hall in
a daze.

We Are the Strangers in Your Neighborhood

Ken Gosse

The tinker with a canker
was a yanker (yes, a wanker),
and for kicks he was a spanker—
oft adorned in women's clothes.

As the good Doc watched the clock,
he would play beneath his smock,
or perhaps beneath his nurse's,
(well, that's how the rumor goes).

The florist is a tourist
in her forest full of flowers;
jungle passions filling hours
till each day, her mind o'erflows.

The coach was once a priest
but deep inside there dwells a beast
which he ne'er allowed to feast—
his lifelong struggle in its throes.

The mayor was a slayer
of all wrong; a true nay-sayer
with a closet full of demons
for each vice that she'd oppose.

As for me, well, I'm retired.
Nothing ever has transpired
that I couldn't tell my neighbors—
using facts that I'd transpose.

Every dawn the sun arose
and we'd don our clean work-clothes;
on our street we wave and greet
our neighbors Bill and Tom and Rose.

Yes, we all have secret thoughts
of varied naughty should-not oughts
which I won't share here for fear
of many lawsuits they'd propose.

So we harbor our impurity
in relative obscurity,
a jaded sense of surety
our secrets no one knows.

less tar

Carl 'Papa' Palmer

us in the bus
carpool lane
riding past her
with cell phone
and cigarette
red BMW convertible
lane-locked in traffic
our eyes meet
reveal to each our dream
she the desire to move swiftly
me wanting to taste the nicotine
from her lips

The Shower

Michael Estabrook

Come join me in the new outdoor shower
in the fresh air under the sun and sky
she waves her arms around
embracing the whole world
who can resist an invitation like that?

He hangs his bathing suit next to hers
the shower is hot the soap is slippery
and so is she but okay time to dry off
and get dressed the children are due back
from the beach any minute

He stands staring at her glistening body
muttering children-schmildren
she hands him a towel and says you're going
to write a poem about this aren't you

Chili Pepper

Sarah Etlinger

There's a chili pepper left over
from the salsa my husband made last night.
So I move it to the windowsill, and in my fingers
it seems so light.
Its body curves, curls
like my favorite whorl of your hair;
(his is so straight—like our son's, too)
it curves lazily
like your twisted legs in my bed.

I am startled that it
shares the same red as my son's fire truck,
the one you stepped on when you last came over.
You hadn't expected it:
your face puckered like you'd eaten the pepper,
the sudden, oily pain a lightning frisson as your feet
skipped across the floor when you rushed,
naked, throwing your socks behind you
before you slipped
between the sheets to me.

I laughed, then—but later
when I found
a stray sock under the bed,
I realized how much it must have hurt.

Prose

Prose

Biscuits

Nod Ghosh

There was another meeting yesterday. I arrived early, parked outside the hall and waited. Scaffolding surrounded the crumbling facade. The building reminded me of a teenager in ill-fitting braces.

I'd made excuses to my wife.

"But Marcus," Helena said. It's always but, but, but with her. Truth is I had to get out of the house, away from her, to clear my head.

I left after dinner and drove around Hagley Park playing Elgar on the stereo.

She was already there. I parked behind her.

She's called Hannah.

Every time I talk to her, I stumble on my words.

I can't look her straight in the eye. She'll know I'm in love with her.

Hannah's car was covered in fine grime. I saw her silhouette inside, waiting for the meeting to start.

Hannah is tall. She's big in every way. I studied the contours of her body. I touched her hugeness with my eyes, though it was hard to capture any detail in that dirty light.

She bent towards the passenger seat and pulled up again.

I imagined her legs. I visualised the ample curve of her bottom, straining at the seams of her trousers. An electric shudder ran through my body. I had to grasp the steering wheel to lessen the discomfort of my erection. From behind, it appeared she was putting something in her mouth.

Oh Lord.

I like a larger woman.

I've asked Helena to put weight on, but she can't or won't. I like to feel the softness of human flesh through silky fabrics. With Helena it is like unwrapping a parcel of bones.

Truth is I'd not been thinking of my wife when we last made love. I'd wished I were peeling back layers to reveal the peach of Hannah's backside.

Oh God.

Partway through, Helena asked if I'd be much longer. Her voice killed the moment.

She switched the bedside lamp on and nudged the pink confection of her nightgown below her bottom. I lay bathed in sweat and embarrassment, as she read her book.

Helena drifted off to sleep.

I was finishing myself off, with visions of Hannah's full weight on me, when Helena woke and berated me for vibrating the bed.

The rain slowed a little. I watched Hannah from my car and I tried to undress her in my mind. Her jaw was working on something. A chocolate bar?

Hannah was licking her lips as she left her car. She entered the building and a shaft of light escaped the entrance illuminating raindrops so they shone like fairy lights.

I followed soon afterwards.

Ann, the organiser was putting chairs out.

Frank, the gentleman who'd tried to gas himself, helped. He's definitely not a full shilling.

I made myself a name badge from the page of sticky labels on the table.

m..a..r..c..u..s.

Ann had laid out a plate of biscuits. I reached for a custard cream at the same time as Hannah. Our fingers touched. I wanted to put hers to my lips and kiss them.

I did nothing of the sort, of course.

"Sorry. You first." She seemed nervous, as she pulled her hand away. "How's your notebook going?" she asked. Our eyes were almost at the same level. I wanted to look away, but remembered what my counsellor had said about eye contact.

"It's, it's −" I dropped my biscuit on the floor and it broke into five or six pieces. I curled my hand into a cup-shape, and swept the crumbs into it.

When I stood up, Hannah was chatting to dreary Frank. I looked for somewhere for the crumbs.

Eighteen of us sat in a ring. Ann introduced the evening's speaker.

It was Hannah.

She read passages from her notebook. It was the same sort as mine. I couldn't concentrate. I kept looking at her fingers curling around the spine of the damn book.

*

"That went well." I said to her afterwards, trying not to stumble on my words.

She took three biscuits from the plate and bit into one.

"Thamksh," her mouth stretched to accommodate the custard cream. A smattering of golden crumbs settled on her skin. Her lips were the colour of Madeira cake.

"I was nervous, but the notebook helped. Thanks for the idea – Marcus." She was looking at my badge. She hadn't remembered my name. I didn't delude myself. We talked about the rain. I pretended we were a couple, just talking, like couples do.

Like Helena and I *never* do.

I suggested discussing our notebook notes before the next meeting.

"Give me your number," she said.

A shudder seeped through me like gravy.

She punched the keys of her phone. Short neat nails. Professional nails. She buttoned her coat like she was going to leave. I wanted to ask her to stay, but couldn't think of a reason.

That damned rain was still falling. It illuminated the dirt on my car. Inside, I sat in the steamy fug, fiddling with the radio long enough to allow Hannah to pull away.

Then I followed her.

I kept enough of a distance between us so she wouldn't notice. I nearly lost her at the lights on Ferry Road.

At Mount Pleasant, she pulled into a side street. I lingered at the junction.

Her driveway was just beyond the intersection. Sporadic raindrops bounced onto my car roof, causing it to sing as I parked outside her house, the place she slept, ate, cleaned her teeth, and bathed. Yellow light shone through the upstairs window curtains.

A thin slice of moon poked through fast-moving clouds. The streetlamps on the main road glittered like a necklace of orange carnelians.

I took my phone out of my pocket and thought of sending her a message. But then I remembered – I had nothing new to tell her about my notebook.

So I imagined her getting ready for bed, and touched myself instead.

Why I am Not a Zen Master

Wayne Scheer

I knew it was there, the eggplant parmigiana from last night's dinner. And that knowledge grew to an obsession.

I had eaten a good dinner, but the memory of this past meal created a lust that needed to be satisfied. There's something about leftovers in a pie pan covered in plastic wrap.

What beauty. The buffalo mozzarella, so white, so pure and pliant, atop dark eggplant, lightly fried and crisp, offset on a fluid canvas of red—saucy, tangy, delicious.

I heard it sing my name while revealing itself to me through its flimsy, see-through veil. I should have resisted such an unsavory siren call, but I am a mere mortal with the appetite of a young man. I could not resist.

I lifted its wrap, inhaled the aromas of Italy, its robust, full-flavored charm. I found myself transported to my youth when restraint represented an unnecessary burden and passion offered the only reason to live.

A handful of pasta called from inside a zip lock bag, longing to be reunited with the red sauce of life. Two handfuls seemed even better.

Would it be so wrong to heat this meal of the gods in a pan with a touch of olive oil?

Ambrosia like this was meant to be savored, devoured. Dare I say it. Loved.

But not at eleven o'clock at night by a seventy-two year old man.

I knew better, but the stomach wants what the stomach wants, and when it involves good food I've always possessed the willpower of a teenager at an all-you-can-eat buffet. The Zen master might eat rice a kernel at a time and be satisfied with ten grains, but I will never master such a feat of discipline, nor do I have any interest in trying.

So I satiated my lust, enjoying my late-night snack with the heel of a crusty Italian bread, light olive oil and garlic.

No butter—it's healthier that way.

The Inner City

Kyle Hemmings

In the apartment, with walls that bend in the heat, Kat is pacing in pink bra, panties, her oversized bunny slippers. She meanders from mirror to mirror, sticking her tongue out, which is meant for me. I mean the reflection. She can regress to a child in a matter of seconds.

It's the end of summer. In the city, birds fly from forgotten attics. Sooty-faced winos rise from manholes. Women are having more babies and the babies are taking over the world. In two days, I will be on a plane to Ohio, to prepare my future in a small college that reminds me of medieval castles and fortresses. Even the birds there know Latin.

Kat kneels between my knees. I'm sitting on an old cushy chair we picked up at a street bazaar one Sunday morning. She sinks her chin near my crotch. Her eyes are wide and tempting.

"You know what I'm going to say, Bugs." That's her nickname for me. Before that I was nothing. Not even a grasshopper in a jar.

"Yes," I say.

She never uses the word, love. It will lead to tragic consequences, complex life stories. For her, it's a metaphysical black hole.

"I'm afraid we'll lose each other."

"I will write and call. I will come home for the vacations."

"Not good enough. Do better. Don't go."

"My parents across the river would kill me. They'd kill you too."

She makes a face, screwing up her nose and upper lip. She reminds me of a close-up of Björk from an old music video where Björk might have been imitating Kat.

I won't tell her that I'll miss her, and the seventeen versions of her. I won't tell her that I'll miss the summer's heavy traffic jams or the breezy echoes of our breaths in the stillness of the night. I loved the fuzziness of waking up next to her, trying to hear her dreamy head hum.

She slides her hands back and forth over my thighs. It gives me goose bumps. It makes me feel powerful, regal, despite my allergies to her tobacco-scented perfumes. Her deep green-alien eyes laser-beam mine. Who's the mysterious panther from outer space?

"Listen, I'm afraid too. The city is full of unfulfilled dudes. Guys with crazy mood-swings. The city is full of other bugs. They can bite and infect you."

She turns her head toward the wall, then back again. She looks reflective, wistful.

"Why don't we go to the roof and see if we can fly?"

I imitate Groucho Mark's jumping eyebrows. Mine are not as thick, but they're not fake.

"Really? Should we get a film crew? Don't we need a license to fly?"

Her eyes are big and sad. Not loveless.

"Seriously, Bugs. It hurts. And it's going to hurt more. I don't want to die like Emily Dickinson."

I feel clumsy and stupid. I fold my hands and look past everything. The way I sometimes do in class when at loss for an answer.

"I doubt I'll die like Lord Byron. Sleeping with every woman who read his poems."

"I got it," says Kat, snapping her fingers. "Let's fuck each other to death. Right here on the floor. CSI will discover traces of us on each other. A mutual homicide, sloppily planned by two unbalanced youths tottering on the wavering line of summer passing into autumn. Let's fuck until our hearts stop. Let's fuck until you have to leave. Let's fuck until we both disappear. Pleeeeease."

I smile at her.

She returns a funny face. A face that masks more mischief. Her eyes hold miniature carefree galaxies where everyone is allergic to gravity.

The news today claims that we will be drawn into a cataclysmic war with North Korea. Dictators across the world are cloning themselves. Everyone lies about disarmament. The way I am Kat's prisoner when she cries after sex. Or when sitting on the subway that will take me back to New Jersey and the fresh lawns of the suburbs. Everything is something else and potentially dangerous.

On this subway, everyone pretends that they wouldn't want to sleep with each other, not even for curiosity's sake. No one wants to give an undercover blowjob. There's a fear of terrorists from every walk of life. But I'm still wearing Kat's scents. I'm coated with Kat. I'm oozing Kat juice. I am no longer afraid of allergies. I twitch as a commuter sneezes. I almost say "God loves you," before I catch myself. The train makes a sharp turn. I hold on to my seat and say "God bless you."

First Date

Carl Chapman

Justin had noticed Regina a few times at school, but because she was a senior and he was a junior he figured the two just didn't mix. But for some reason, today she just sauntered up to him in the parking lot and told him she needed "to talk," and would he ride with her.

Being a standard male hormone-charged teenager, Justin obligingly climbed into her car. As she drove, he checked out Regina's long red hair, freckled face, and rather nerdy looking glasses, along with her breasts which seemed more than ample in size. Bucket seats were the norm for most cars, but Justin noticed that Regina's car had one long seat in front that would allow them to get close to one another if they wanted.

Like that would ever happen, he thought.

Regina smiled and told him he was cute, and then turned to drive into the country which was easy to do since they lived on nothing but backroads in the country.

Now things were getting more interesting and just a little weird.

Eventually, she stopped the car and parked at the side of the road and turned to him. "Look," she said. "I like you, and I want you to like me. Do you like me?"

"Of course," he responded.

"Good."

With that, she kissed him hard and then moved her hand to his crotch and started stroking him, making Justin's mind race.

His body wanted this, but his mind kept saying something's not right here. He wanted to go home; but felt he didn't have the willpower to say anything. Besides, if it got out that he chickened out he'd be totally humiliated by the guys at school. It was a small town and an even smaller school. Everyone would know in a matter of hours he chickened out. It wouldn't be long before they'd all be talking about him and it wouldn't be good.

Regina removed her beige blouse and matching beige bra and Justin got his first look at a woman's breasts; they were round and rather full, and her nipples were quite pink; not too large, more of a handful as the guys in the locker room would say. She placed his hands on her breasts, and sensing hesitancy quickly stroked his crotch with her fingernails.

Soon, Justin was too excited to stop what seemed destined, or perhaps even planned.

Slipping off her jeans and panties, Justin got his first complete look at a woman. She had a beautiful red tuft of hair that beckoned him, and before he could think, she had pulled off his jeans and briefs and climbed on top of him.

It wasn't long before the rush came, but with that rush came fear. I'm not wearing a condom, he thought. Possibly sensing the fear, Regina increased the rhythm. It's too late, thought Justin. I can't stop now. He guessed this was what lust was but wasn't sure since he'd never really experienced it before, except with his own hand. It was all happening so fast that even though it was pleasurable, it was also rather terrifying. He was surprised he could stay hard at all. He guessed his body could operate on autopilot if given the proper motivation, and her body was the proper motivation.

Afterwards, Regina pulled off him and slid back to her side of the car, quickly grabbing her jeans to cover herself.

"Was it okay?" she asked.

"Yes, of course," he replied.

"We better get home," she said, as she quickly pulled her panties and jeans back on, giving Justin a little more time to view her breasts, a lasting memory as it were.

Still confused about everything that had just transpired, and starting to feel embarrassed, Justin pulled on his briefs and jeans, struggling to do so while in the front seat of the car. Funny how it seemed so effortless to get them off, yet so difficult to put them back on. Why did everything feel so clumsy and awkward now?

Regina drove him up to his car that was still parked near the high school.

"We'll talk later," she said and quickly drove off without another word.

Justin climbed into his car and sat there for a moment. He couldn't help but feel he'd just been raped. Yeah, he'd wanted it, but he hadn't wanted it the way it happened. He also couldn't help but feel he'd just made a terrible mistake. He knew he would see her again and dreaded what would happen next. He'd just experienced his first time and it wasn't anything like he'd imagined or wanted.

'Tis the Season

Paul Beckman

Tradition calls for each of the family to get two gifts. Denny, the oldest sibling, passes out the gifts calling the name of the person getting and hanging on to the gift card. The person getting the gift has to guess who gave it and why. This is as much anticipated as getting the gifts. It's a fun after feast activity, since no one has the energy to go outside and play.

They were down to one gift and everyone knew it was for the unlovable husband and stepfather, Johnny. Me and Denny hoped it would be a tie since their stepfather refused to ever wear one.

He opened the box and inside were seven other boxes; all of various sizes. Each was labeled. Johnny opened the one with the "Gluttony" tag and inside was a picture of Johnny reclining by the pool, large belly overhanging and the picture taken from the pool that made the belly look even larger than it was. He was sleeping, head tilted to the side, drool escaping from his mouth catching on his hairy arms. He held a can of beer in a death grip on his leg.

"Mary Ann," he guessed, calling out his wife's name. The family laughed and booed and told him to select another. He grabbed one wrapped in red and opened it. "Anger" was written on the card.

"You people may think you're having fun at my expense but let me tell you: I don't find this fun or funny and I don't give a rat's ass. William," he guessed and a chorus of no's sang out.

One after another befell the same fate until he got to the last one wrapped in lace. "Lust," Johnny said and opened it to find a picture of him looking through the hedges at their neighbor Tara sunbathing topless. The picture was taken from the upstairs bedroom so there was no mistaking what Jerry was doing.

He slammed down the box. "You're all a bunch of no fun perverts and I'm not playing anymore." He snagged the card from Denny's hand, prepared to lambaste the guilty giver. He saw that it was signed from every one there so he hefted himself up and walked out to the garage where he kept his stash hidden.

Since You Asked

Robert Carlton

There are several good reasons why I so often use the shower for this purpose:

1. First and foremost, because this is the one place that affords the necessary privacy for the act, no matter time of day or how many other people may be in the house.

2. Because on the nights when your best friend comes over for dinner I do not want to sit around all evening trying to hide a boner.

3. Because that one woman at work is so damnably adorable that I can barely contain myself until I get home.

4. Because on those alternate weekends when your teenage daughter visits, all I can think about is getting her naked, and I feel no guilt.

5. Because my favorite cocktail waitress has big tits and is happily married.

6. Because, despite the lack of personal acquaintance necessary to support a realistic fantasy, images of certain actresses flicker through my thoughts constantly, including, but not limited to, six TV detectives, one TV personal assistant, five TV lawyers, two movie super heroines, and one sidekick in a kids' series on PBS.

7. And finally, because sometimes I think I might even still want to fuck you.

Like I said, there are several good reasons why I use the shower for this purpose so often.

Lusting After Victoria

Larry Lefkowitz

Victoria removed her clothing without any hint of embarrassment – unlike Kunzman who did so also, most uncomfortably. She finished first. Kunzman, to his considerable embarrassment, was briefly delayed by a stuck zipper – he felt himself an actor in a Yiddish comedy; Victoria feigned not to notice, though a slight movement of her nether lip betrayed her and Kunzman thought he discerned the pale fire in her eyes suddenly go out. Standing thus naked, waiting for him to finish undressing, Victoria stood there, in all her nakedness. Seeing Victoria standing naked in all her splendor, and reflecting on his own naked form in comparison, Kunzman remembered Lacan's query whether the phallus is still a master signifier in the present order of Western society.

He began to gather his clothes from the bed where, in his unavailing haste, he had at first put them, with the purpose of laying each article of clothing neatly on the wooden hanger which stood in the corner of the room. Victoria, grasping his intention, arrested him, in a voice of impatience, or was it disdain? "Throw them on the floor, Kunzman."

He recalled ex-wife's Nitza once characterizing him as "cautious to the point of self-parody."

His hesitation apparently got on her nerves. "Nu, what are you waiting for?"

"Godot," he didn't reply.

"*Shem zikh nit*," (Don't be bashful), Victoria urged him.

Stop thinking so much, Kunzman admonished himself. Concentrate. The success of the evening depends upon it. Hardly propitious was his suddenly recalling the admonition: "A man is not too old until it takes him longer to rest up than it did to get tired." As counterpoint, he recalled the Yiddish saying: *Az men lebt derlept men* ("If you live long enough, anything can happen"). It had been a long time since his physiology had been subjected to such (pleasurable) stress. He had the odd sensation that no reciprocal physiology was taking place on the part of his partner, even though the outward manifestations of the act were taking place *de rigueur*.

In the wall mirror, Kunzman caught himself and Victoria intertwined. 'The enraptured beast, doomed to one day die, as so many are.' No time now for Nabokov's gentle reminder.

Although on one hand (after so many years of being *sans* the commodity) sex with Victoria was pleasurable; on the other hand, it was marred with worries on the part of Kunzman – worries beyond the basic worry of whether he would succeed physically with this fabulous, but moody, beauty. He feared a *gresile*; he feared a *fortzele*. It seemed the act, somehow, brought Yiddish expressions to his mind, or, somehow, the sight of her did (he knew that she, like him, spoke the language). He noticed her *poopikel*, her *nezlile*, her *tsitskes*. And what did she notice of his? He thought of Zeus's mistress Semele, just before she was burned to a crisp by a bolt of lightning hurled by Zeus for seeing her divine lover as he really was. But the hell with it, Zeus or no Zeus, lover divine or less than divine, Kunzman concentrated on carrying out the physical pursuits at hand, murmuring to her almost without being aware of it a series of endearments: my *ketzele*, my *oystere*, my *kroynele*. They ceased abruptly not because of what Kunzman perceived as Victoria's mocking half smile or the martyred line of her brows, or even her displeased murmured "*Oy*" at the first endearment, "*Oy vey*" at the second, and "*Oy vey is mir*" at the last, but because of her telling him that he was a *maskenspieler*. Kunzman sighed, reflecting: why were even his most intimate moments invariably accompanied by a flavoring of vile farce?

Perhaps this feeling was connected to another one that Kunzman often had – that he was not living his life so much as *narrating* it. The curse, no doubt, of the writer.

And after Kunzman had "worked" and had more or less acquitted himself in his love-making with Victoria – *me dreyt zich*, as they say in Yiddish, for good measure throwing in, after the fact, a few more whispered endearments, "*mayn zeeshkayt*," "*mayn ketsele*," and even "*mayn katchele*" (though Kunzman was fully aware that the latter was an especially egregious oxymoron as applied to Victoria) – and, having wiped the sweat off his forehead, exhausted like a *hon nokh tashmish* (a rooster after the hens have been serviced) yet immersed in the euphoria of successful release *post copulam carnalem*, his floating stage of post-coital bliss disturbed momentarily by Yeats' "A shudder in the loins engenders there/ The broken wall, the burning roof and tower/ And Agamemnon dead" and destroyed finally by Victoria's chattering away – unlike Kunzman's ex-wife who promptly (and now, thought Kunzman, mercifully) slept following the act, Victoria seemed to be stimulated to speech and was going on, a sound like the buzzing of bees in his ears.

"You're not listening to a word I said," she said. Kunzman had learned that a 'conversation' with Victoria could be an onerous proposition. It was hard to be a passive conversant with her – to listen, as was his wont. Victoria prodded, asked questions: "You understand?" "What do you say to that?" and so forth. You had to *pay attention*. A physically wearying process. When it was over, Kunzman felt as if he had just finished a wrestling match or a five-set tennis contest. "Are you listening, Kunzman?" she would say if his attention flagged. If more exasperated, "Are you alive, Kunzman?" "Barely," he would whisper to himself. For his sin of "not listening" on the present occasion, he immediately apologized. "Oh, don't apologize," she admonished him, "I can't stand men who say 'I'm sorry.' Just shut up." Nevertheless, he kissed her cheek and, resisting the urge to borrow the endearment "fire of my loins" from Humbert of 'Lolita', opted for murmuring a Yiddish tribute to her love-making.

A Most Desirable Girl

Abha Iyengar

Sitting in the breezy café in New Delhi's Meherchand Market, her slim fingers are working hard, kneading the soft braided bread, like flesh, before breaking it up into small pieces, rolling each piece between her fingers to make it more malleable. She then dips one balled up piece into the hot lentil soup on her table and pushes it hard into her open mouth. Her lips closed, she now closely sucks at the ball of bread in her mouth, and I watch her cheeks pulling in and pushing out as she consumes the piece. She finally swallows it all with a sigh.

The other balled up pieces lie waiting. I suddenly feel I am one of them. I want to be kneaded, rolled, dunked and sucked. She is young, ordinary, nondescript. I am old, lonely, withered and gone.

I feel the sap rising as I watch her. Suddenly, she becomes a most desirable girl. If she does this to food, surely she could do the same to me.

I walk up to her and say, "Hello!"

She looks at me and nods. Her mouth is full.

"May I sit?" I ask.

She swallows what she has in her mouth. Then she looks at me and says, "What do you want, Grandpa?"

Bless Me Father

Robert Iulo

"Bless me, Father, for I have sinned. It's been one month since my last confession."

But what a month. I had just started in an all-boys Catholic high school, and it was my first time going to confession there. I had learned about a whole new category of sins. In elementary school, having been taught by Sisters of Charity, I didn't consider myself much of a sinner. Starting at about age seven or eight, we were encouraged to go to confession every week. I often had trouble coming up with any sins to confess. An easy one was cursing. What we kids considered cursing wasn't quite the same as what the Church thought of it. It usually went something like this:

Father, I cursed.

What did you say?

I called my friend an asshole, and I said fuck five times.

Did you use the Lord's name in vain?

No, Father.

What you said is profanity. It's not good but not as bad as using the Lord's name in vain. Don't do that. For your penance say three Hail Marys.

As long as the nuns taught us about sinning, it wasn't too bad. But in high school, instead of Sisters of Charity, we were taught by Christian Brothers. All of the sins the nuns were too modest to mention weren't a problem for these guys.

At our first religion class, we were given a book called *Nothing Below the Belt*. It began with a picture of two fighters in a ring with the caption, "The best rule is the boxer's rule; nothing below the belt." Our religion teacher, Brother Patrick, went through it in excruciating detail. It dealt specifically with the Sixth Commandment and adultery. I knew about adultery, and there was no way, at thirteen, that I had committed it. According to Brother Patrick, it wasn't so simple. He had a whole book to explain there was a lot more to it. Moses might have gotten that Commandment in five little words, "Thou Shalt Not Commit Adultery," but in the millennia since, the Church interpreted them to mean much more, summed up in just one word – lust.

He started with "impure thoughts," a mortal sin, with its obligatory eternal hellfire. And for what? For an adolescent boy enjoying thinking about sex. How were we supposed to steer clear of those very natural thoughts? By praying, of course. That was the best Brother Patrick could come up with. It didn't work.

After he felt he had solved that problem for us, he went on to "nocturnal emissions." I at first thought it had something to do with car engine exhaust but what he meant were wet dreams. We were in our early teens, and all of us had and looked forward to having these pleasant emissions. Did he expect us to suddenly stop them? "This isn't something you can consciously avoid," he said, "but if you wake up during one of these dreams, say a decade of the Rosary." That's ten Hail Marys.

So with wet dreams out of the way, masturbation came next. The solution – just don't do it. You got an erection? – Pray. It's as easy as that. Studying hard and playing lots of sports helps too.

After a few more classes, he finally arrived at actual, physical girls (not only thoughts about them). He started with "prolonged kissing." That's something more than the kiss you give to grandma. He didn't indicate a time limit and never mentioned tongues. What he said was, "Prolonged kissing can lead to much, much worse things," and he ended the subject there. Some of the kids in the class still hadn't engaged in prolonged kissing, but I had, always hoping it would lead to much, much worse things.

He said we might be more familiar with his next subject, "improper touching," as "necking" or "petting." These were 1950s terms he assumed were still in use. We called it "making out." He used countless words to tell us what body parts would be improper to touch, but he never said exactly what they were, leaving us guessing.

After a few weeks in Brother Patrick's class, I found the bottom line was that anything to do with sex was a mortal sin if procreation within marriage wasn't the end result. And I wondered how, with such strict regulations, Catholics could manage to procreate at all.

I was now ready for my first confession in high school, with all of these new sins committed before I knew they were sins. I decided to simply face it, tell the priest everything and get it over with as quickly as possible. It began with my usual venial sins. You didn't go to Hell for all eternity for those. Instead, you did a stretch in Purgatory. The priest's response to this part was, "Try to be good and don't do that again." Then I started with my "below the belt" mortal sins. He questioned me in excruciating detail about each one. He grilled me for what seemed like hours. I couldn't wait to get out of that dark little box. At the end, he gave me the biggest penance I'd ever gotten. So big that the rest of the class had to wait for me to get back to school. And what was the result of all this Catholic education? Did it put me off sex? No, it put me off religion.

What You Want

T.C. Mill

It begins as a feeling of discomfort. Warmth crawls beneath your skin, a heated glow around your fingers, tension in your cheeks. It gets to the point where you can't even sit in the same room with him, because sooner or later your body and mind snap tight, contracting with what you want, an internal orbit around unspeakable things.

It's difficult, because you've been seeing each other now for three months.

It's especially difficult today, at the end of Memorial Day weekend, the first solid seventy-two hours in each other's company.

And the most difficult part of all is that by this morning, you know you want to keep doing this. Every hour, every twenty-four hours, every seventy-two—every instant of the fifty-two one-hundred-sixty-eight hour packages in the year. You want to spend them with him.

If you can without wanting to fly across the room and...

It's one thing to say he's so handsome you could punch him, but what do you really want?

Because it can't be that.

Last night, when he took your ringing phone off the coffee table and handed it to you, his bent, broad shoulders and long, lean back and something about the points of his knees through his slim jeans made you want to make him crawl.

These sparks of aggression aren't driven by hatred, or even by anger—after seventy-two hours with most people you'd have felt angry at some point—except he inspires a kind of frustration in you. A hunger for more. It's not sexual lust, though you feel that too. Instead it's some purer, impure desire.

Not to drive him away, finding your old succor in solitude—it's an urge to attack, not defend yourself. A way of coming close, invading him the way you've always been so afraid of being invaded. As if it makes a difference, being the aggressor.

To step on his kneeling back and push him flat on the ground. Kick until he turns over—not hard; you feel it wouldn't take much force. What you want is to put your hand on his hammering pulse, delicately, to reach deeper, carefully, to grip the shuddering, shattering heart.

You want it so much that it doesn't feel wrong. But you want it so much it scares you. So much that you can't think about consequences.

You could strike until bruises show, letting your own palm go numb from impact. You've made a few testing strikes on your thighs, on the fleshy part of your upper arm. You haven't been able to give yourself more than a sharp white star of sensation followed by lingering soreness. No marks. But God, the eerie satisfaction as you feel your fingers connect with your own skin, the warmth and softness of it yielding under the force of your blow.

What if it was his? Flesh, that is, not blow. It's a one-sided fight you're thinking of.

His footsteps scuff the kitchen linoleum, drawers rolling open and shut, along with a sound like a distant, tinny marching band that is really him whistling under his breath. You imagine the way his longish hair floats in cloud formations stirred by his every gesture.

You want that hair pulled tight in your fingers.

Pulling your legs up, you curl in your seat.

"Hungry?" he calls.

"Yeah."

His body, trembling, opening under your nails. You want him moaning beneath you, bleeding against your teeth.

You close your eyes, glowering through the lids at these fantasies. You wish they were more mystifying than they are. All your life you've wanted to be able to act without restraint. You've wanted to be dislikeable—snarky, superior, cold, even cruel—but not disliked. It almost stands to reason that you're here now, wanting to commit murder without anyone dying.

Wanting to not-quite-murder him precisely because of how close you are to loving him.

If this is love. Probably not. It's only wanting.

You sit, shaking with it, muscles straining, fingers digging into your arms, toes kneading the cushion on the seat of the chair.

Why now? Why here? Why him?

"I'm hungry," you say, choking back a confession of how much you want to eat him up.

All those consequences you're not ready for—the confront-ation, the clash, or worse yet, the intimacy of him knowing how much you want to devour him. And accepting it. And—maybe, even—asking for it.

His whistling returns, a little louder now, the band marching nearer.

You try, if not to want something else, at least to think of something else. Calming, soothing things. Spring days, not too hot. Cool running water with no flavor. Always the turn to nature. You were taught to think of nature when you needed prettiness.

He's pretty, naturally, but not what you're supposed to think of now.

Think of other lovely things. Like being in love. Which you aren't. Would be easier if you were.

Or not. As if you know.

From the kitchen, thunder rattles. Pan lids slide against each other, cymbals crashing with a flourish as the rest of the marching band vanishes. Instead of whistling, he shouts. You've never heard him swear before, and the stream of profanity is astonishing—how much more happens in his mind than he's ever shared with you. How many vile things.

He stops for breath, a long hiss of it through teeth. You imagine broken skin, scratched white or red, as you hear him riding out the pain. Your heart pulses with it. Then you jump up and come running. "Are you okay? You're not hurt?"

Absolute Trouble

Len Kuntz

You were there and then you weren't.

The house and the bedroom and the bed and the lamplight were there and then they weren't.

The world spun and sputtered and then it wasn't there anymore either.

You came home angry. There were tiny beads of sweat above your lips and brow. Your chest was blotchy, stucco pink. The breath coming out of your nose sounded like a hairdryer set on LOW. As if it was nothing, as if you did it all the time (though you didn't), you stripped in the kitchen without saying a word, sighing often, but you left your panties and stilettoes on. Then you flung your hand and said, "Get the fuck in the bedroom. Now," and you meant it.

I went.

You carried a satchel with you that looked heavy. You said, "On the bed. On your stomach." You said, "I want you butt-naked, now." And you meant it.

I obeyed.

You tied my wrists to the bedposts with satin scarves I'd never seen before. You did the same to my ankles. You tied them tight, as a serial killer might, as if you'd done this before. You blindfolded me. You leaned down with your breath in my ear furnace-hot, and said, "Disobey me and there will be absolute trouble. Got it?"

I did my best to nod, though my face was smashed against the bedding like a crushed boulder.

Half-whispering, half-snarling, you told me in precise detail what you were going to do and how you were going to do it. You said, "This is what captivity looks like, what torture looks like, but really it's more like a second cousin of freedom. Understand?"

I didn't at all, but I tried to nod anyway.

You were surprisingly gentle, then you weren't. There was some kind of frayed whip lashing my back. There was searing heat, liquid heat being drizzled, being doled out in dime-sized drips, but there were also lumps of ice which you ran across the back of my thighs and along my buttocks which had seen most of the whip. There was nibbling and biting. It seemed as if you were trying to carve a code into my skin with your teeth. You licked my neck and your tongue had never felt so wet or so long. You grabbed my hair and yanked it, asking, "Are we good?"

I'd never seen this side of you. It seemed impossible. It was fantastic. I felt we were on the cusp of some kind of liberation, the way you said we would be.

When I nodded, you slapped the back of my head and bit my earlobe, which was just more fantastic, and I came for the third time since we'd started, a sticky, wet pool sopping the sheets beneath my groin.

In the bedroom, even though I couldn't see, there was nothing else but me and you—you, the slave owner, hell-bent on punishment, and me your captive. I never knew the reason for it, what I'd done, or if this was some masochistic side you'd always kept secret, though I didn't fucking care.

You took me from behind with something slick and long, malleable and unreal. "I've always wanted this," you said, chuckling. "I bet you have, too."

You were thrusting as you said the words, but I tried to nod anyway.

The room smelled like us, the sweaty parts of us, the odd odors I had come to know so well, some slightly pungent, yet erotic exactly because they were slightly pungent. I couldn't see, yet the room still swirled each time you touched or bit or hit me with something rough. It was penance, punishment and a kind of deliverance all engulfed in one, and I loved it.

Your wet mouth swallowed my right ear. It felt like being eaten by a seal. You said, "It's important that you understand when we're done here, I'm gone."

I didn't understand at all, and still I nodded. I assumed you were joking and that this was all a fantasy.

Your last, brutal kindness I cannot tell anyone. Or maybe I can. I'm still on that bed, in that room, with a swath of lamplight warming skin that I cannot see. I'm still waiting for your return. I'm burning up, shivering and shrivelling, yet I am so fucking alive.

Come wound me again.

Allure

M Pauseman

Not all superheroes wear capes. Cliché, I know, but then again, not all villains wear masks. Human psyche is an amazing and complex thing. Everyone remembers the names Jeffrey Dahmer, Ted Bundy, Charles Manson or Fred and Rose West, but does anybody remember the name of the detective in charge of the investigation?

I first fell for Jennifer Christmas when she was Alison Dupree. She witnessed the murder of her family from outside the living room window. She arrived late to her parents for Christmas dinner and heard the muffled scream. Her husband, her two daughters and her parents, tied and gagged. Shot one by one while she watched from outside. Even with mascara running down her face, I knew I loved her. It was almost an hour before she spoke to me after she came running into the station. What she described moved me like no other crime I had investigated. All witnesses shared an image that cannot be taken away from them, and they all told their story in a similar fashion, but not Alison. Something made her story stand out from the millions of witnesses I had spoken to throughout my career.

I visited daily, trying to remain professional, but she knew I loved her. She confided in me, and we spoke about everything. I felt that she knew me better than I knew myself, and yet, I knew nothing about her. I loved that mystery, the one case I could not solve. A failed marriage leaves a mark, but nothing that can compare to being widowed in such a way.

Jennifer's smile pushed me over the edge. We kissed. It was a kiss that would take my mind away from everything that happened next.

Jennifer asked me constantly about my work, about murder scenes I had been to and about killers I had questioned. She knew how to make me share every detail. Disfigured bodies, rapes, bludgeoned heads and slit throats all became fresh in my memory. It had been twelve years since I first walked on a crime scene as a detective, but she made me remember it like it was that very morning. I remember the smell of iron from the puddles of blood, the remaining paint fumes in the factory, and through the heavy cape of death, the smell of her perfume. Allure, by Chanel. Jennifer bought that very one.

Looking into her eyes was like looking at Peyto Lake, which brought back memories of my teenage days, visiting Canada with my father. It was my father that inspired me to become a detective. After his death, I swore who no more children would have to go without justice. I had not cried at his funeral, but talking about him to Jennifer made me cry for all the times I never did. She held my hand in hers. Like worms wrapped in a silk cocoon, my fingers felt at home. That night I stayed with her.

*

I never thought I would be in the back of a car. Not with my hands behind my back and regret heavy in my heart. She blew me a kiss from the other car. I could not blow one back.

*

I brought copies of photographs back for her to see. I thought she would retreat behind cushions and the blanket. I was wrong. Each photo was from a more horrific crime I had worked on. Each photo brought her closer to me, closer to the edge of her seat. I never had before and never have since had such passionate sex. The danger of my job made her lust for me like I have never experienced before. I heard that adrenaline could be confused with love, but I knew I loved Jennifer more than anyone I had ever loved.

I finished late that Wednesday, but I still went to visit her. I could hear her moan and scream. I rushed in to the bedroom. She was laying on the bed, naked and surrounded by the copies I had brought her. She told me to prove my love to her. I began to use my badge to get away with it, first videoing it for her to masturbate over or to play in the background while we had sex, and then I began to take her with me. She would hide and watch from the shadows whilst I took petty criminals, homeless and prostitutes through extreme levels of pain. She lusted over the blood, over me. And I too began to lust for blood. The smell of Allure constantly at the scenes.

Nobody remembers Patricia Lazarus for the criminals she caught and convicted. Nobody remembers Patricia Lazarus the heroine. Patricia Lazarus, together with Alison Dupree, killed over ten people. That is what people will remember. They will twist some details and say we had sex in the puddles of blood, or that we would take selfies as the victims took their last breath. We will know that isn't the truth. Patricia Lazarus, detective turned murderer. That is the only truth I know.

Demon Heart

Stephen V. Ramey

The blackflies are thick this time of year in Michigan's Upper Peninsula. The undergrowth is thick too. Walking a path is like negotiating a series of grasping hands intent upon dragging you down. I don't know why Melissa and I come here. We're hardly Yoopers, having moved away as seven-year-olds when our parents divorced. Twins, boy and girl, mirrored half-heart birthmarks on our buttocks, hers the left, mine the right. Something pulls us back year after year, something deep and dark and wild.

Ahead, the path splits. The left branch leads into tangled brush. The right skirts a swamp.

"Which way," Melissa says. My eyes go to the curve of her hip. I feel it in my mind, that layer of yielding flesh, the deeper skeleton, thighs so firm and meaty.

"You ask that every time," I say.

"I forget."

"Well, I forget too." Memory is a fickle thing up here. Events sink down inside you and disappear, leaving a hint of stench.

She follows the swamp path. Sunlight slants down, a blood of fire across my bared arms. Mosquitoes swarm. Melissa slaps a few, then gives up. We trudge in silence, me trying not to imagine her buttocks raised high. *Not here.* I have no idea what it will look like, this sacred place we seek but never find.

We pass a rotted log, its sodden brown pulp overgrown with mushrooms. A butterfly settles on the path. Melissa stomps it dead.

She collapses to her knees. "You know this is wrong. We both know it's wrong."

"Get up." My body trembles. Lust? Rage? Does it matter? I pry her from the ground. Wince morphs into defiant grin on my sister's lovely face. In this moment she would murder me if she were able.

I throw her forward. Grass sprinkled with flowers waves from either side of the path. The smell is a flavor in my mouth. I want to swallow my spit until it fills me up.

Melissa wipes the back of her hand down her leg, turns it, strokes her inner thigh. A blackfly bites her arm, leaving a well of blood. She looks hopeful. "Maybe if we do it here...?"

"Keep walking." I shove her into motion.

We enter the tree line. Shade washes us with cool. Rather than extinguishing my lust, this new contrast hones it like a knife. The forest buzzes with energies. *Hallowed ground.*

I pull Melissa around and slap her hard enough to feel her teeth. She sprawls over a sapling onto hands and knees. I rip my shirt over my head, spike it down, unbutton my pants.

A fierce grin comes over Melissa. She springs, a fallen branch in her hand. *Thwack!* sounds through the forest. The branch breaks across my back.

I go down, and she's on me, clawing, tearing, growling deep in her throat. A red whirlwind sweeps me. I turn beneath her, pull her face to mine. We flip. She's under me now.

"I love you," I grunt. She spits in my face. We wrestle, bodies throbbing to the beat of a demon heart. Twigs scrape. Rocks prod. I tear at her clothes. She grabs my hair. When we have spent ourselves, we lay panting on the forest floor, legs and fingers entwined.

"We're like animals," Melissa says. She cups her breasts. "It's disgusting. We're disgusting."

I slap my blood-sweated chest, and think of our childhood, parents who loved each other until they suddenly didn't, the schools we attended, the bullies we endured. Always the odd ones out, the outcasts. We had only ourselves.

"This is what the world has made us," I say. "What else can we be?"

Togetherness

David Miller

Most often they would read to each other at night, but today in the midst of a storm that had followed a long humid blast of summer, they read in the late afternoon. He preferred the late afternoons, and he was particularly fond of a potent storm. It heightened his senses as he felt the rain clattering against the window, the branch of a tree scraping and stammering arhythmically.

They would alternate, each would read for five or ten minutes, there would be discussion, then the baton would be passed. Today he was reading Walt Whitman, and she, Elizabeth Barrett Browning. It was not always poetry, and there were no firm rules that informed this ritual. Fiction, non-fiction (invariably history), articles from the newspaper could sometimes feature. He once read out the instruction manual that facilitated the operation of a Japanese hand-held miniature vacuum cleaner. *Step 7, 'The fluff gives you the dust to disappear'* became a cherished mutual memory. On occasion, she would read from an old recipe book; meals that they were most unlikely to ever consume – 'Rabbit with Prunes and Pine Nuts' being one such example. Unlike many couples, they had grown to love the sound of each other's voices.

As she read Aurora Leigh, and as the wind-driven rain continued to lacerate the window, he began to speculate on whether she might step out later that night. He would tire easily these days. It was not at all uncommon for him to be deep in sleep by half past nine. There was no expectation for her to do the same, and he was well aware of the intensity of her drive: an insistent amorous drive that could effortlessly shift to a surge. She would often take the initiative. She was unusually assertive. Could fuck like a man. He knew her drive all too well, and he was perfectly alright with it, semi-encouraging her dalliances.

Of course they had their acquiescent conventions. She never brought anyone home, never stayed the night. Her lovers were all in their twenties, half her age. They never lingered, nor did she require them to. It was a purely physical release, and they most certainly never read to each other.

He would at times recall how flawless their sex had been. How exquisite and unique. Untameable, adventurous, limitless, elastic. He had long ago exhausted the superlatives. There were instances, (for her discretion was such that she would rarely initiate this sort of conversation), he would elicit details from her. Fragments from her nights out. Initially he thought this may have been a way of reassuring himself. To determine that there was no lover capable of taking her to some stratosphere where only they had been before. He soon realised that it was a different reassurance that he sought. That she was treated with respect, that they had brought her happiness. This is what truly drove his questioning. At the very least, he owed her that much, and he was thoroughly convinced that there could be no couple anywhere capable of attaining and capturing their brilliance.

There had been no jealousy, and there had been no insecurity. He wished that there had been no guilt, but it would be disingenuous to believe there had been none. It sat there latently in his solar plexus, a thin diaphanous coating. A minute membrane that evoked that fateful night. *Sure, he would meet his* old uni mates at the bar. *How long had it been? And he couldn't wait to show off his new bike. New? Almost an antique. A MK III Norton Commando. A collectible. Their eyes would light up. And they most definitely did.*

Two beers in, someone bought him a scotch. Make this my last, he determined. Then the jugs of beer arrived. It's Happy Hour! Not for me, he told them. You can't go now. Reckon I should. You can't. Not in this. Thumbs pointed toward the window. It's pissing down. One more then that's it. Just while the rain eases.

Then time grew jumbled. It was late. Another jug. Maybe two. No one was counting. It had been a while. Outside now. Soft spitting rain. Still. Cold. He was leaning on his bike. Mounting. Astride. The cool air would wake him up. Sober him. Key turning. Purring. Igniting. Minor explosions. Backfiring. Revving. Suddenly out on the road. The slick road. Homeward. Alive. Spontaneous. Reckless.

He took a corner a little too fast. Overcompensated, and then just as quickly regained control. Then the light ahead. No warning. Turning amber. Panic. Brakes locking. Sliding. Lost it. No redress. Scraping. Dragging. Holding on. With desperation. From nowhere. A minivan. Off-white. Sliding. Forever. Hurtling. Inescapably. Inevitably. Into blackness.

*

After a time he regretted the loss of his bike more than the permanent loss of feeling in his legs. With time, the period of adjustment became less arduous. Intimacy had evolved. The holding of hands, the kissing, the massage, the meandering conversations, the reading aloud of their favourite passages. It was a true intimacy. It heightened his senses.

*

He had lost all track of time, having briefly dozed off since dinner. His head turned slowly toward the bedside clock as the

LED numbers seamlessly transformed from 9:09 into 9:10. The room was dimly illuminated by the bedside lamp. His index finger was still wedged inside the book, marking his place.

She was standing before the open drapes gazing out into the unremitting torrential rain. Her fingers dislodging buttons as she vacantly disrobed. "You'd think there couldn't be any more rain in those clouds," she mused.

In time she was naked, reaching for her sky blue nightie. She slid in under the sheet beside him, and lightly kissed his temple. Her hand sought his, fingers interlocking. A barely perceptible smile formed on his face. She would be staying in tonight, and he felt so pleasantly content.

Lusty Cruise Ship Pirates

Paul Lewallan

Hannah Mueller stood at the bar, her scandalously tiny new bikini carefully hidden by a white long-sleeved sun shirt. She clutched her novel in one hand and the drink specials in the other as she anxiously stared toward her daughter on the pool deck.

"Rocky start, huh?"

"I beg your pardon?"

The man in blue swim trunks and red parrot aloha suit was tall, tan, and slender. "It's only Day Two of your cruise, and your daughter has already gotten on your nerves."

"How did you know?"

"This morning I was two rows back on the Conch Train tour of Key West, then I went to Red Fish Blue Fish for a cold beer and conch fritters. You walked in a half-hour later carrying shopping bags and arguing." He held out his hand. "I'm Kip Kettering. Let me buy you a drink."

"Why?"

"You're an attractive woman alone in a bar. Cruise regulations require it."

She smiled weakly and shook his hand. "I'm Hannah Mueller."

He pointed to the romance novel she held, *Lusty Seas.* "Cruise research?"

"Hardly. It's a bodice ripper with oversexed women and lusty pirates."

"Lusty pirates are the best." Kip was a decade younger than her with pale blue eyes, high cheekbones, and an unpretentious smile. "Now about that drink…."

"I'm not a drinker. I went to a Christian college and married a pastor who shunned alcohol."

"And will Reverend Mueller be joining you on this trip?"

"No. I divorced the cheating son-of-a-bitch two years ago." Hannah picked up the drink specials. "What do you suggest?"

"Sex on the Beach."

"I beg your pardon!"

"Sex on the Beach: cranberry juice, orange juice, peach schnapps, and vodka."

Hannah glanced back to the pool where her daughter Ruth was chatting up a handsome silver-haired male in a Speedo. Ruth graduated three years ago from North Dakota State and worked as a CPA in Fargo. She was the one paying for the trip.

"All right," Hannah resolved, "buy me one of those."

When Kip returned, he placed four drinks on the bar. "Two-for-one special. Can't turn down a bargain." He handed Hannah a tall glass with orange slices and a straw, then raised his gin and tonic and toasted. "To lusty women and the pirates who court them."

"If only," Hannah laughed. She sipped the drink appreciatively. "Very fruity."

"So," Kip asked cautiously, "who's the handsome old stud with your daughter?"

Hannah sighed. "That's Bill Kellerman. We shared a table at breakfast. He wasn't going ashore, but suggested we meet him poolside when we got back. He's a widower."

"Well preserved. Definitely pirate material." They watched Ruth stand up and shed her over-blouse revealing a tiny purple

110

bikini. When she walked to the pool's edge and dove in, Bill rushed to join her. "So in Key West you argued about him?"

"Is it that obvious?" From the expression on Kip's face she knew it was. "He was very attentive at breakfast, to both of us. He suggested drinks at the pool, and Ruth agreed before I could decline." He nursed his gin and tonic, waiting for her to finish. "She insisted on new swimwear in Key West."

"And you argued over the scandalous bikini she bought?"

Hannah nodded, and took another drink. "Ruth dared me to buy one that matched."

"Pirate bait?"

"Definitely." She leaned in and confessed, "I married the first and only man I have ever had sex with." Hannah finished her first drink and reached for the second. "Ruth wants me to find out what I've missed."

"The swimsuit is a good start." Kip turned back to the pool. "Focus on Bill for now, then work your way through the passenger list. Save the crew for last."

"It won't be that easy."

"Let's find out." He took the drink from her and set it on the bar. "Let me take your wrap."

She shook her head. "I can't do it."

"Of course you can, and you want to do it. That's why you bought the bikini." He reached for her sun shirt. "May I?" Hannah opened the single button on the wrap and Kip eased it from her shoulders. "Pretend Bill's a pirate."

Hannah used her thumbs to adjust her bikini bottom and kicked off her sandals. "And I'm a lusty wench."

Poolside Bill lay on his stomach with Ruth straddling him. When her mother suddenly appeared beside her, she stopped lathering his back with suntan lotion.

"Stand up," Hannah said sternly. "You missed a spot." She pointed to the area just below his right shoulder blade.

"I thought you…" Ruth sputtered as she stood.

Hannah took her daughter's arm and pulled her aside. "Have you done the front?"

"No, I…" Ruth glanced over to Kip.

"No matter. I'm here now." Hannah knelt beside Bill and slapped his butt. "Roll over." Hesitantly he did so. "Oh my. What we have here?" She pointed to his erection struggling to climb out of his swim trunks. "Houston," she joked to Kip, "we have a problem." She ran her fingers up the length of his cock. "One easily resolved." She looked up at Ruth. "I'm going to take Bill to our stateroom and help him out."

"I, ah…," Ruth stammered.

"If you'd rather do it yourself, I'd understand," her mother offered. "I mean you caused the problem."

"No, go right ahead, if that's what you want."

"Definitely." She stood up, grabbed her wrap from Kip, and started dragging Bill off the pool deck. "Give us an hour before you come change for supper." She called back to Kip. "Would you join us? The Main Dining Room at 7:00."

"I'd be honored."

After Hannah and Bill left, Ruth turned to Kip. "Your idea worked."

"Of course. This isn't my first cruise."

"How many drinks did you buy her?"

"Two, but one would have been sufficient. She wanted to do that, she just needed an excuse." He eyed Ruth grinning at him. "You have any more of that lotion?"

"I thought you'd never ask."

What Remains

James Wade

In the clearing, surrounded by a mix of pine and oak, the building's steeple rose toward the sky. I stared at it, the cross at the top fighting off tree branches as they twisted in the first wind of autumn. I watched as the sun abandoned its supremacy, its light consumed by the gathering storm. I felt my father's hand on my shoulder, firm and guiding. I allowed my gaze to fall.

Candles filled the darkness. Small flames gave birth to great shadows, and on the walls arose demons. They craved entrance into our holy hall, but I knew our faith would keep them at bay. The wooden pew was hard on my bottom, but I welcomed it. There was no room, I knew, for comfort and faith to coexist.

Only seven families remained, where once there had been dozens. Those who left had refused to see the truth. Brother Gregory was overcome, they said, afflicted with ill-begotten perversions of the gospel. But I knew better. I could feel it. Brother Gregory was our salvation made flesh and bone.

As the demons danced between the nails and slats, Brother Gregory smiled and nodded his head. He stood tall behind a plain-carved pulpit. Rendered from loblolly, it held sturdy and erect as Brother Gregory grasped it with both hands.

"Dear brothers and sisters," he began, closing his eyes and continuing to smile, "our Lord Christ has blessed me with another vision."

A few of the elders murmured their praises as Brother Gregory began to rock back and forth from the pulpit.

"Yes, He came to me in a dream, unclothed and bare-bottomed. He was, as He was on the Cross, devoid of hubris and vanity. He bled from wounds abounding. Suffering, brothers and sisters, as was his purpose. Suffering, as is ours."

I watched him speak, his lips full but soft, despite the strength and command of his voice. Though many had questioned his youth, his ability to lead was apparent. In front of the congregation he spoke of fire and blood and sacrifice in a tone so fierce it was undoubtedly our Lord God himself delivering the message.

I longed for his approval and attention. The light from the raised window behind him gave his silhouette the same glow I imagined Michael having as he struck down Satan's armies. When I sinned, I sinned to his image, to his voice, to the thought of his touch.

"There can be no salvation without suffering," Brother Gregory continued, "and who are we to deny the pain we have been gifted by our Lord?"

"Amens" and other confirmations were scattered through the pews.

"But I sense, there is conflict here," he said, his smile turning into the hostile face of judgement. "There is someone here who has not embraced the suffering the Lord God Almighty has called him to endure."

I felt my face begin to flush. There was thunder, perhaps from the storm outside, or perhaps from the Hand of God himself. The windows shook and the shadow demons scattered. I tried to breathe, but Brother Gregory continued.

"Satan is the sloth who refuses the responsibilities given to him by God. Yes! Lucifer, is the fallen angel who lets greed control his every thought. The gluttony of self-satisfaction is what invites these demons and their Master into our lives. But we can cast them out, cast them back to hell!"

The building began to tremble as I fought back tears. The image of Brother Gregory's pale skin entwined with my own battered down my defenses like a small artillery unit laying siege.

"Who among you has harbored sin? Who among you has become a bellwether for the darkness? Confess now! Confess, dear soul, lest your wickedness become transformed into the very hand of Satan himself."

My mouth opened, but there were no words. My hands reached toward my chest, then clawed at my throat. The door to the sanctuary was thrown open by a howling wind and there were gasps as the candles extinguished their light and the demons were released into our world.

"Yes!" Brother Gregory cried, his head tilted back and his arms outstretched. "Come forth, ye troubled soul, and I will cast your sin from thee! Confess! Confess and be washed clean!"

"Lust!" I shouted, dropping to my knees as the rain began to pound the roof of the chapel. "I have sinned and it is lust and it is too strong for me."

An elder brought the doors back to a close and slid the bolt into place. The sounds of the storm were once again relegated to the world outside of our walls, and Brother Gregory's voice fell to match the faded volume.

"Lust," he repeated. "And at such a young age."

He came down to my family's aisle, sliding past my mother and father, both of whom seemed stricken with shock. He laid his hands on my shoulders.

"Lust," he said once more, quietly, moving his mouth toward my ear. "And what must we do to atone for such a sin?"

I looked into his eyes. They were brown, but something more. Something sinister, but excited. We stared at one another, until a smile crept across my lips.

"Pain," I whispered, realizing everything and nothing at once.

"Pain!" he called out to the congregation.

The doors were again flung open, this time by my own father, and the families followed us outside. The rain soaked my hair and the water ran into my eyes as I braced myself against the fading paint of the church wall.

"What is your sin?" Brother Gregory cried as the dogwood branch came down against my backside.

"Lust!" I yelled in return.

"And what is your atonement?"

"Pain!"

"Your sin?" he demanded once more.

Then, "Your atonement?"

Sin and atonement. Lust and pain and lust and pain and, when I looked into his eyes again, only one remained.

Hands

Angelina Taylor

Rough, dirty hands. Mechanic hands, farmer hands, welder hands, miner hands. Stubby fingers, palms with calluses, nails stained with motor oil and grease. Hands moved up and down her body. They grabbed at her, took charge of her. She lay back and closed her eyes, feeling the men exploring her body as much as they wanted. They mapped it out, documented her and found new places. Bobby discovered her neck, Steven discovered that spot on either side of her hips. Russ, lying next to her, had found her earlobe. Russ' snore interrupted her fantasy; cutting through the ghost of a tingle she recalled travelling through her body in her youth. The thoughts dug her nails into the bedsheets and beads of sweat formed on her upper lip.

The hands of these men, Bobby, Steven, David, James, Ben, Martin, Guillermo, Marcus, and countless others whose names were long forgotten, were saved and catalogued inside her mind. They were, of course, altered; enhanced by fantasy and the unreliability of the human memory, but she preferred it that way. She had edited out the awkward removals of intricate clothing, the clinking of teeth and numerous 'misfires', resulting in irreversibly stained sheets. These improved memories served her well at night. She was alive, swimming in recollections, feeling a familiar heat inside her, spurred on by the songs that reminded her of the past.

Her stomach muscles tensed as Elton John's *Rocket Man* began playing through her headphones. The iPod or iPad or iPhone her granddaughter had set up for her contained a complete list of her sex songs. No one else knew what the songs meant and she'd never tell. There wouldn't be a single person besides her husband who wouldn't be repulsed at the thought that she had ever had sex.

She rolled over and looked at her husband; the sounds of the CPAP machine cut through the feeling inside her as it pumped air into his lungs and prevented him from dying in the night. The sagging skin on his cheeks melted over the elastic of the mask, almost covering it entirely and his mountainous stomach blocked her view of the alarm clock. She looked down to her own stomach; it was not much better. There would be no hands on her body, in her body, anymore. But if her body's time was up, why did she still want it?

No longer did she wish to wear high heels and drink alcohol; neither were missed. But the roughness of a man's hands bringing her to the point of climax was something she never thought she'd be forced to give up.

When was the last time it had happened? She remembered the first time well enough: Billy Goldman, 1945, front yard of her parents' house while dinner was in the oven. They'd wanted to celebrate. She'd walked back in and sat down to dinner as if nothing had happened. In reality though, she was a changed woman.

The *last* time though, she couldn't remember. She couldn't have ever known it would be the last time, could she? Had her husband known it? If he had, perhaps it would have been more special, more memorable. Does anyone know that the last time is the last time? How does it phase out? Do people just... forget to do it?

118

Her husband coughed violently and clawed at his mask in his sleep. She sighed, held it over his mouth until he stopped thrashing and answered her own question: a loss of attraction. She didn't find big stomachs and breathing apparatus attractive. She found the cashier at Woolworths attractive with his youthful face, long hair and disinterested manner. She found Hugh Jackman attractive, even when he was singing and carrying on on-stage. And she'd have a go on Larry Emdur, especially post-weight loss. But not her husband, not anymore; the only person with whom she was technically allowed.

There was, however, one thing that could not be taken away from her. She rolled to her other side and opened the bottom drawer of her bedside table. Her arthritic hands struggled to open the old biscuit tin labelled 'family photos'. Under the lid lay the final element to her outlet that could be conveniently set to the rhythm of Russ' CPAP. It could do something for her that her hands no longer could.

Neighbourly

Peter Lingard

I was atop the ladder cleaning out the gutters when I saw the guy next door, in his conservatory, apparently making out with my wife. I had enough sense not to react but to quietly descend. He, Fred, lost his wife around a year ago and I imagine he felt lonely now and then. I'd told him about my trouble-and-strife over beers at the local pub. I must have spoken so highly of her that he decided to sample her delights. Lust'll do that; like it did for me all those years ago. Like a good fish, he firmly took the bait.

My wife liked to think of herself as liberal-minded and it was therefore characteristic of her to provide poor Fred with some companionship. On reflection, it might have been my wife who initiated the action in an effort to comfort Fred. Sometimes one can't be sure who's initiating what; not that it mattered in this case. I don't consider myself liberal-minded, but I decided to cede my wife to Fred. I walked to his house, around the back of it, and knocked on a pane of cracked glass.

"Glad to see you two getting on so well." They both jumped, surprised and embarrassed. "It's okay, guys. Don't fret. It's all alright by me. I suppose you'll want to help May collect her things, Fred. Best do it now, before I change the locks." I meant it. May's been miserable for a few years and I hope, for both their sakes, she attains happiness once more.

One of her oft-quoted maxims is, one man is as much a bastard as any other, so she might, if she fails to appreciate my altruistic motive, complain about my magnanimous gesture. But who would she complain to? Hardly Fred. It'll have to be one of those inner things; kept submerged; unable to let out. Perhaps she could unload to a psychoanalyst, or one of those types. It's possible she might harbour hard feelings against me for a while but it'd be in Fred's interest to soothe away the anger she so enjoys. If he's successful, he'll delight in her until she feels settled and able to let her true self re-emerge.

What Bella Wants

Joseph Szewczyk

Welcome to the parking garage of Arizona Charlie's hotel and casino...little hunchback dwarfs pulling a cart, one leg dragging behind them, the handle coming undone until all that's left is a piece of luggage minisculing, flambing around forgotten, like a ragged mistreated child shrinking off into the sunset.

Inside the casino itself are souls going 'round and 'round, trapped on some sort of hellish carousel ride where the only possible way off is to win big: the one hopeless pull of the handle, the one horse that falls over the line, one more free drink served by a waitress who resembles something out of the JC Penney catalogue circa 1967 with faux pink stuffed butts, torn pantyhose and a tattered one-piece swimsuit, a body once like Zelda Fitzgerald's, now not even to be recognized or desired.

So, here we are, all the Damned who couldn't make the trip. I thought to myself, this isn't the American Dream, this is the left-overs, the umbilicus, the slough'd off what it used to be, the people who couldn't make it; this is the purgatory, forever damned to be eating 25 cent cheeseburgers and drinking dollar margaritas.

No, not Oscar Goodman's vision of Las Vegas: the tall blonde and tan bombshell, sculpted perfectly in Venus' image, holding a margarita glass in one hand, and saluting with the other. This is the hellish, warped Van Gogh vision of Las

Vegas, the one too ugly to show on the Strip; populated with people not quite fit for the glitz and glamour of the City. What happens in Vegas, stays in Vegas mostly because they are not welcomed anywhere else—the shambling mounds that infest the off-strip casinos; wild sunk-in eyes; leathery flesh hanging off their faces; bones supporting the protruding mask-like thing which now passes for a smile; slobbering mouths filled with rotted teeth ready to sink into anything that gets in the way. The land that time forgot, and for a reason.

Yet inside you can be transported back into forgotten days with everyone singing Elvis tunes; the oxygen-pumped rooms keeping vital organs running; their bodies well preserved with piss and smoke, like the images presented to us by Boris Karloff. Pickled people, not Egyptian royalty, haunt the bingo halls. Whatever happened to their souls? God's own Creation mocking Him in silence (in a silence only broken up by the blips, flips and dwips of the machines).

Beyond the machines awaits something of the Flesh. Casual runnings of the night, desires not bound in money, but in connection. Connecting to something, anything, a shrivelled soul reaching out blindly to the world, grasping at anything, trying to hold on, as the fingers fall away; a cursed grip that either lets everything flow like water or crushes the very object of desire. Petals into sand.

This is where we find Bella, and, if you value your heart, where, for the present, we must leave Bella. Bella, the lost child, all grown up and still searching for a love that is no more real than any of the phantoms inhabiting (stalking) the casino. This is Bella's Boudoir—this hotel room poking out shyly trying to hide away from the casino's main body—the lure of a voice, the twinkle of a nose and glitter'd eyes beckoning the damned, not those devoured by the Greed monster, but the ones left battered and torn; wretched remainders of one heart's filthy sin.

Love is a Sin; God knows this and that is why He turned His back on us.

I met Bella once, but back then she called herself Annie; she was sweet—weren't we all—somewhere along the line things got twisted. It started all so simple. But Now isn't Then. I saw her once in the Now; I saw her as Bella; she was wearing an impossibly tall high-heel, her long doe legs shaking with every step. I said, "Honey, honey, how the fuck do you walk in those?"

She looked at me and smiled, "Darling, walking isn't what I do in them."

The Education of a Young Gentleman

Charles Jacobson

Outside Richie's bedroom, the Virgin Mary stared down at me from the wall. Like a fool, my hand stuck on the knob—this was the sacred retreat where Larry had filled us with lies and exaggerations. Slowly I turned the knob and pushed the door open. The warm, moist air was heavy with perfume and semen. A small form sprawled across the bed.

A low, seraphic voice called from the darkness, "Larry?"

My breath escaped me. I jammed my hands in my pockets—too late to retreat and too dark to gauge her senses. My ears knew nothing of her except that she was well beyond my experience. In my best Larry, I uttered, "Yes ... "

She turned over on her back. I stepped in and closed the door. She knows what to do.

The coverlet my mother made for Richie lay crumpled in the corner. My hand trembled while I slowly pulled back the sweaty bedclothes. Why is she so far from the people who care for her? Getting even with her husband or single for the night? I was not in my right mind until she spread out and said, "Here. Let me look."

I dropped my drawers. She splayed her pussy with her fingers. I wouldn't have to lick or remove anything.

She opened my shirt and clinched my neck with her fingers. Stirred by her touch, I shut my eyes and sank into her unguent warmth. She arched her back and let out a moan. Her red beans were cookin'.

I had lost all sense of time and direction when I pushed away from her embrace and blundered out, stumbling over a pair of shoes.

Only Richie remained in the avocado-green living room; everyone else was gone. Bishop Sheen's *Way to Happiness* and a pair of yellow gloves lay carelessly on the coffee table together with a few pieces of jewelry.

It was after two o'clock when Richie reclaimed his bed. Her sudden appearance from the shadows did not detract from my previous estimate—little more than five foot, chasin' thirty—some body, a blue-dyed rag around her head and a high, womanly chest puckering Richie's open-necked red flannel shirt.

She stopped to gaze at the fine rain falling on the front lawn before closing the honey-colored drapes and seeking me out. The yellowish light from the lamp fell upon a face that had retained much girlish beauty. I took her scent and felt her breath—we were almost touching. She lit a long cigarette and stared at me with cloudy gray-green eyes. An arabesque veil of smoke drifted back into her face. She straightened a tangle of dusky hair and bent forward with half-parted lips, placing her warm, moist fingers over my eyes with a nonchalant flourish. "Am I young enough for you?"

Her playful whisper demanded an answer. A hot blush came to my cheek. "You ..."

She put a finger to her lips and moved against me. "Shhh. I like what you did."

I put down my beer to taste tobacco and stale mint on her tongue. I kissed her throat and slid my fingers onto her breasts with no displeasure. After lighting a second cigarette with the first, she sipped the top off her drink and led me downstairs. All I could think of was, season well and top with oysters. All I could remember was white-velvet breasts, a c-section and painted nails digging into my back on the cold-hard floor.

We passed out in a tangle next to our spilled drinks. When the light filtering in through the casements roused me, I dressed silently and climbed the stairs in an unsteady haze to go to the loo. Instead, I caught a glimpse of a curving figure in black staring into the mirror, spike heels, cigarette in one hand, eyeliner in the other.

A pair of headlights pulled up in the drive.

Shouts at the front door!

"Herald Angels?"

"No—Larry."

If She Knew

Andrew Grenfell

Friday

"Please say hello to Jessica. She'll be working in our department for the next three months." All eyes, and then again. Dark green dress, business-like, hugging. Skin of golden porcelain. Don't stare. Long luscious brown hair tamed in a sturdy ponytail. Someone is saying words. Don't stare. Sunset lips the colour of roaring embers. Don't stare. Curve of her mouth, a hint of cruelty at the edges. Bell-like voice. Lashes.

Never understood until now how a face could launch a thousand ships. But those cheekbones, those cheekbones!

Saturday

Try not to stalk on social media. Who is she, really, this woman? Body suffused with yearning, likes of which. Here she is smiling sitting atop a hill, hair swirling, anguished sky pressing down. A ski trip. With a friend, arms around, bare arms, bare shoulders. The same person in the centre of another life. Cradling a tabby cat. More of the girl inside. Wearing a silly hat. Then *that* black and white photo in a dress that follows every sweet curve. A knowingness in the eyes. What have you seen, my love?

Sunday

The storm shows no sign of depletion. Merciless fantasy, mist of longing. Fires to warm the bones.

Monday

This is ridiculous, can't behave this way. Shower, cleanse, swept clean. Maintain discipline. Coffee and a sense of purpose. Staid morning meeting with the usual suspects: beefy Huan, sandy-haired Gerard, willowy Clementine –

All goes to hell as soon as she's standing right next, oh my. Speak to her, be welcoming, effusive. How to operate this body, this brain, this mouth, with this self-consciousness? How to hide this? Pretend to be someone else, someone who doesn't crave touching the camber of her hips, her sumptuous mystery, her envious youth. Oh my. If she ever knew.

Tuesday

This will never end. Everything seen and touched is flared and alive. Concentration, distraction. Search for a glimpse of her. Imagine the morning light coming through the window, in bands upon her naked body. The agony of her nipples.

Wednesday

Working together, picking through a spreadsheet. Together. She takes no notes. Quick intelligence or nonchalance? Intoxication of proximity. Adopt a casual but winning manner. Meet her eyes. Explain and smile. Skirt hesitant just above her knee. Blood red lips beckon. Every ounce of will not to reach out a hand and touch her leg. Can no more explain this than stop the moon.

Up close she is delicious creamy perfection. Relaxed, but is something contained within? Women and their secrets.

Friendliness of the collegial. Give to receive. In the workplace, we pretend we do not have bodies. But oh! If she gave herself.

Thursday

Can't sleep. Ache of distance. Don't think of the swell of her breast, of what she might cry out. Oh, treasure. Can't sleep. Drink in the swell of her breast, think of what she might cry out.

Friday

Casual dress. Her floral blouse caressing, washed out jeans. Light mood in the office, drinks and canapes after. Noise and consumption. Speaking, joking, laughing. Favourite things, preposterous hypotheticals, ironic opinions. Everything attributed to her, the palaces proscribed for her personality, once merely glimpsed, now upheld in soaring divergent colours. Soul fullness. Seconds where it seems possible for all dreams. Of course showing no signs of the hundred imagined violations done to her. The gathering moves on to a classy pub, the family-burdened having peeled away.

Relaxed, tipsy, slurry, drunk, touch her shoulder, she smiles. Clink glasses, conceit of tradition. Attention turned away to another male colleague – it's Gerard. Never stand a chance. As if the tide of desire could even... Buy another round, convivial cocktails. Oh, he's touching her arm and laughing, leaning in to her, ostensibly to hear better over the crowd thrum and music. God, he's almost leering, buffoon-like. Whatever. Look around. Brassy stale women with garish cleavage, all the wrong people on the prowl. Gleam of affluence. And where is she now, cherished Jessica? Nowhere to be seen. Whatever. Too loud, too close, too hot, so out into the bracing night air, unsteady stars aswirl. Outside, outside, alone,

alone. Big patch of blurry grass, fall with half a laugh, stare up at the sky, all those indifferent stars. Let it all ebb away, leaking down into the cold earth with a snake's smile. To be empty, closed eyes. To feel the bliss of nothingness, free of the fizzing of lust at last. Coursing of blind chemicals.

Open eyes to a new world ablush with purity, finding her face looking down, hair waterfalling, a tickling river, and the fire of her lips inches away.

Valentine's Special

Edith Knight

The moon was our only witness; actually, our accomplice. If it hadn't approved, it would have hidden behind the clouds, but no, it shone down on us in all of its glory, illuminating the smooth contours on Napery's naked body. I traced my fingers round her small breasts and her nipples perked up in response. She trembled. I became hard for the second time.

"Oh Kwame," she moaned, rolling over towards me and giving me more access. I continued caressing her. She sighed in pleasure with eyes closed as she reached out to fondle my erection.

She half opened her eyes. "How long before they get here?"

"In about five minutes." I increased the pressure on her nipples as my free hand wandered down to her thighs. Her wet entrance made my member strain against her thigh. I held myself in great control; I had to wait for the perfect time.

The best part was yet to come. For right about now, my wife was making her way towards this path; in tow with her lover, of course. Napery and I had selected this spot as they had to pass through to access the car they had abandoned behind the thicket. What better way to surprise your spouse than her catching you in the act with another woman as she's coming from the same act with another man.

I wasn't planning on hitching with Napery after this, in fact the only reason she agreed to this crazy plan was because I assured her I would not ask anything in the form of commitment from her, besides the sex of course. We didn't love each other; but our lust had always overpowered us and so when I found out my wife was cheating two months ago, I had sought her out after three years and my body still responded magnetically to her.

I heard footsteps approaching from a distance as I lowered myself into Napery. This was the grand finale; losing myself in the writhing woman below me, I closed my eyes and rode her wildly.

What's in a name?

Jeffrey Weisman

I've often wondered if people with the same name share similar characteristics or traits.

Some years ago when I ran an advertising agency in Chicago, I heard about another agency whose president had the same name as mine. I called him one day curious to see what we had in common besides our names and our professions. I left a message with his secretary. He never returned my call.

Back in those days, as a single man always on the prowl, I would try to sit near attractive women in public places such as a local bar.

Soon after my unreturned phone call to my namesake, I stopped by a favorite bar on the way home. At one end of the bar I saw an older gentleman nursing his drink. Midway down the bar I saw a pretty, even attractive, woman with long dark hair. I didn't want to make my interest too obvious so I sat two stools away from her.

As I sat down, she looked at me and smiled. I returned the smile. A few minutes later, we looked at each other again. I smiled and asked if she frequented this bar. I had never seen her here before.

We began a conversation: how we liked this bar; our appreciation for this part of town; where we worked; where we lived; the usual break-the-ice social dialogue. I asked her name. She said "Judith."

Then she asked my name. I answered "James." "James what," she asked.

"James Walker. Call me Jim."

She paused and had an incredulous look on her face. "You're joking," she said.

"No, that's my name."

She began to laugh. "What's so funny?," I asked.

"James Walker is the name of my ex-husband."

"No, now you're joking."

I sat there dumbfounded. After more conversation, I realized that her ex-husband was the same Chicago advertising president who declined to return my call.

"What was he like?" I asked. I wanted to know if having the same name would have meant we had similar personalities.

She described her ex-husband as a bit smug, arrogant, and though attractive, not very giving. She even shared that she wasn't sure why she married him. In my opinion he certainly didn't sound anything like me.

We talked about our lives in Chicago and general social conversation. And with each lull in the conversation, we came back to the coincidence of two men in the same business with the same names.

The more we talked, the more attractive she became. She had good looks to start. Her dark brown hair in an Arlene Dahl/Lauren Bacall style fell over one eye. She looked to have an athletic body, as best as I could see from her sitting on a barstool. She had crossed her leg and the muscle in her calf showed nice definition.

Beyond the physical features, her conversation and opinions and ideas aroused me. We clearly had something in common besides the name of her ex-husband.

As we finished our second round of drinks, I asked if we might get together again. "Sure, I'd like that," she replied.

We made plans to meet again on Thursday night, same bar, same time.

As she departed, we shook hands. I gave her a kiss on each cheek in the European manner. She reacted with pleasure, not cringing as an uninterested or shy woman might.

We could have asked for each other's contact information, phone number or email address. But social strictures tended to rule against that. We just made do with our promises to meet.

The next three days passed by very quickly. I looked forward to seeing her again. I felt like a teenager with a high school crush. How youthful. How wonderful. Fate had brought the two of us together.

I arrived at the bar early that Thursday evening. Full of expectation, I kept turning my head every time the door opened and people entered. None of them Judith.

She was late. Time passed by. After two hours of nervous waiting, I reluctantly realized she would not come.

Having had such high expectations, I felt disappointed and depressed and I ordered another drink. All of my fantasies dashed.

I so longed to see her again. And because she did not show up, I began to feel a sense of lust for her. Unrequited love, out of a sense of desperation, can lead to fantasy and with it lust. So it did with me.

Of course I returned to the bar the next night at the same time and even on the same stool. But once again, no Judith.

I went back to the bar the next seven nights. Still no Judith. So perfect yet so far away.

I wonder why she did not show up to meet again. Perhaps she was married and just playing along for the social exercise fun of it all. Or perhaps one James Walker in her life proved sufficient.

I never did get her last name. I tried to find a Judith Walker on Google but to no avail.

I still go to that bar occasionally, always with a little bit of hope.

I wonder if women named Judith have the same characteristics.

A Vacation
from Depravity

Jenean McBrearty

"After the war," Antoine said, "I'll do something dangerous. Rob a bank. Highjack a truck full of cigars." He was lying on a chaise under a palm tree on a Havana beach. The other tourists thought him crazy for sunbathing in the shade; tans were evidence of leisure.

Daphne motioned the cabana boy to bring her another Gimlet. "I don't understand why the ladies love you."

"I don't talk much in the bedroom. Conversation is tedious with the politically uninformed and the drunk."

Was he counting? This was only her third afternoon cocktail. "How many Nazis are there in Cuba, do you think?"

"Enough to make Roosevelt want to count them."

"Do you think Hitler is going to invade Miami?"

Antoine – formerly Captain Anthony Walker – stifled a laugh. The Nazis were scouting landing fields. "Wars end eventually. Every German in uniform is hedging his bets on escaping to safe havens. They'll have to go farther south, of course, if they hope to evade the Jewish avengers."

She took a baby-sip from her glass. His face was scarred but his body was still disciplined, and that made for long, full evenings when he was so inclined. He hadn't touched her for months, convinced she'd fallen in love with someone else. "Are you going to gamble tonight?"

"I'm working on a sure thing."

"The Signora has a message," the cabana boy interrupted, and handed Daphne a note.

"Excuse me, Antoine. I'll see you later," she whispered as she kissed his cheek.

As instructed, the boy came back. He leaned over, dropped a key into Antoine's lap, and whispered, "Major Hausman. Room 704."

"Gracias, Roberto."

Poor Daphne Pierpoint. Killed in the battle of the sexes. Perhaps by a jealous wife? *Was* there a Frau Hausman? The thought crossed his mind last night when he saw the Major winning big at *punto banco*. What part does chance play in life? Dresden had been firebombed into oblivion. Was Frau Hausman there, smoldering among the charred bricks and wondering if she would remember the names of her dead children? Did the Major send her any of his winnings?

Antoine checked his watch. He'd need to shower after suffering through the hottest part of the day doing nothing except looking desirable in a pair of white shorts and a sleeveless tee-shirt. He'd need to eat, too. Perhaps meat from the bullring. And he'd have to decide which he hated more: Pierpoint or fascism. It mattered because the second target had approximately three seconds to move out of the line of fire, to roll off the bed, and evade an assassin's bullet.

Antoine opened his still-sighted right eye. His patch-covered left one still hurt sometimes, but he never let that interfere with seizing the initiative when opportunity presents itself. The OSS would be none the wiser. Today, he'd gamble with the lives of two people, and the odds were a hundred to one in his favor that one of them would die. Which one? He'd let chance decide. Heads, his faithless lover. Tails, Karl Hausman.

He flipped a next-to-worthless peso and watched it tumble through the air. It landed with a dull thud. He turned his head to the left, and saw it had landed straight up between the grass and the leg of his chaise lounge. He walked to the bar and ordered a Bloody Mary.

*

He wore dark pants and a red flowered sports shirt. Good for hiding blood spatter. Just in case. Cologne covered the smell. He'd often escaped notice by simply maintaining his tourist identity in the midst of post-incident panic. Yes, men noticed his face, but turned away to avoid seeming rude. The women noticed too, but he turned away to avoid their instincts to mother.

He took the elevator to the seventh floor, turned right and entered the second door on the left to wait for the inevitable. Daphne and her Major would end up here eventually. Three P.M. or three A.M. it didn't matter. The first one to use the bathroom would be the first to go.

As it happened, it was the Major. No sooner had he closed the door than Antoine pulled piano wire around the throat of the soldier whose luck at cards and love had just run out. Attempts to struggle only hastened the collapse of his windpipe. That was the beauty of murder by garrote.

As he lowered the body to the floor, he heard knocking and Daphne's hesitant voice. "Darling, are you alright?"

He drew his luger, opened the door and fired at her chest through a folded towel. She fell back, wide-eyed with terror as death descended upon her. He fired again straight through her adulterous heart, wiped the luger with the towel, and threw it out the window into the hedges below.

He hated manual kills. Guns were quicker and less personal. He casually strolled to the elevator, but the adrenaline blasting through his heart kept shouting run! run! His muscles engorged with energy. Denying both flight and fight, he felt like caged electricity as he rode downward. The elevator stopped at the third floor. A maid carrying clean sheets glanced at him, then shifted her eyes downward as the door closed behind her; his hands closed around her neck.

When next the doors opened, he was in the underground parking lot. He sprinted up the ramp to the road, up the stairs to the lobby, through the stairway up four flights, and down the hall to his room, panting. Sweating. Spent. Revolted by his own bloodlust, but physically relieved.

He showered, and dressed for cocktails and dinner served on the palm-encircled patio. He'd hear tangos and mambos and tales of the unfortunate deaths, guests and staff alike. There would be an inquiry, but everyone knew that in wartime lots of people died. A German Major, and an American tourist. Perhaps they were spies, Antoine suggested. The rape and murder of a pretty maid? Perhaps she had a jealous boyfriend. And Roberto? Perhaps a robbery gone bad.

Antoine stayed another week in Havana. He deserved a real vacation after the death of Agent Pierpoint, his superiors said.

Mr Jackson

Christine Johnson

In the beginning she liked Mr Jackson. Even though she was eleven and he was much older. Around the ladies, her mother said, he was full of beans.

"Bit of a flirt. He thinks he has the knack. But respectful, never out of line."

She watched her mother smile, accept Mr Jackson's light-hearted compliments and banter. But, despite her young age, she felt he always kept his final words for her. Telling her in front of her mother how she had grown; teasing her over how pretty she was. How 'those big sweet chocolate eyes of hers' would all-too-soon be enough to melt any man's heart.

At first this made her shy. Talking to him was like leaping over a row of tricksy hurdles. She feared she might trip and fall, never sure what might come up next. Although he made her laugh – there *was* something clownish about him – sometimes she wondered if he went too far; doing little things she knew somehow weren't right.

That cap he wore. He would shift it to one side, setting it at a raffish angle. Make a funny face, pursing his lips in her direction when no one was looking. She felt his hot breath on her skin as he came closer. Having landed his kiss on her cheek his big hand lingered on her waist, moved up her ribcage. It seemed impolite to resist or say no. It was only playful tickling.

She imagined her mother advising her: "No need to worry. That's just Mr Jackson. The way he is. Unconventional yes, but hardly disreputable."

And she had even heard her father talking sympathetically to her mother about him. He suggested Mr Jackson deserved their pity. Like a character in a fairy tale, it sounded as if he was held prisoner by a witch, one with considerable sway over him.

"Poor bloke, I gather she's a battle-axe, one who keeps him on a short leash. A miserable old biddy, so they say – hard and scheming – enough to frighten any man. It must be a relief for him, to drive out on his pick-up rounds, spend his hours working away."

So over time she came to accept how Mr Jackson fussed over her.

Until one day, catching her alone, he slid his bulky hand between the buttons of her blouse and under her singlet. Cupping her almost non-existent breast, with one thick finger he touched her nipple. He stroked it.

Her heart lurched. Hotness spread throughout her body. She felt a strange, prickling sensation as if her blood stopped, turned and was retreating the way it had come. Her blushes deepened. And all the time, confused, she looked at him. Eyes wide, lips parted, she didn't move. Mr Jackson pulled away his hand. Without a backward look he climbed up into the driver's seat of his truck and drove away.

The next time the vehicle came to the farm after Mr Jackson had touched her someone else was driving. She heard the reply to her mother's inquiry.

"Jacko? He's taken a sickie."

It was two more weeks before she saw him again. She hung back; watched him loading his vehicle, by his serious face and uncharacteristic silence.

"Mr Jackson?"

She spoke shyly. He looked at her.

"You're feeling better?"

"Yes."

"You're not – angry – with me?"

"No."

He hesitated and then, as if to prove it, invited her to climb up into the cabin of his truck. As she settled, nervously gripping the edge of the seat, her hand touched something. She glanced down. On the cover of a glossy magazine a pouting, busty beauty leaned forward, exposing bikinied breasts like full udders ready for milking to the eye of the camera.

Embarrassed, she looked away. Mr Jackson stretched across her to stuff the magazine into the glove box. With him so close to her, the cabin of the truck felt hot, his body bulky. Rather than moving away he remained beside her. He placed his hand tentatively on one barely visible outline of her breast and then moved it across to fondle the other. His hand lingered.

Later, she tried to recall what happened next, but whenever she reached back to touch it, fright exploded in her. Everything seemed to take place so rapidly it was as if flesh fell from her bones, leaving her exposed, a see-through carcass.

He grasped her. Moved his hand down onto her bare knee and slid it under her skirt, up along her thigh. Consumed by lust he tugged at her underwear. He shoved her down flat on the seat and lay on her. She felt tiny. Crushed, she remembered crying out, calling him by his name.

"Mr Jackson? You're hurting! Please, Mr Jackson."

Pain, it hurt more, stabbing, tearing her, and then it was over. He was pulling out of her, short of breath, slithering back behind the steering wheel.

She was shaking, close to tears. "Mr Jackson?"

144

"Listen, don't ever tell, you promise!"

"What?" Her voice wavered. "Yes, promise, cross my heart."

He insisted. "This is our secret. Understood?"

She heard the threat behind his last word and nodded. But his attention was already elsewhere, in his lap, as he fumbled with his clothes. A noise nearby and up jerked his head. He looked out the window. Glancing back at her, he swore.

"Bloody hell, cover yourself! Quick."

Her mother stepped out into the yard. Mr Jackson snatched his cap up from the dashboard, set it at a jaunty angle. He gave her mother a wave. She waved back.

Distracted, she didn't notice her daughter, terrified, bleeding and ashamed, climbing down from the passenger side of the truck and slipping away.

Home Delivery

Steven Carr

On his way out the door, George kissed Claire lightly on the cheek.

She closed the door and brushed back her unruly mousey brown hair back from her face with her fingers. She turned her back to the door then leaned back against it and let out a loud sigh. Kicking at the hardwood floor with the tip of her fluffy pink slipper she stared with disinterest at her disheveled living room. A strand of dust hung from a blade on the ceiling fan that spun around, wobbly. The screws holding it to the ceiling were coming loose. Listlessly she walked away from the door and on her way to her bedroom she kicked the empty potato chip bag that lay on the hallway floor.

In her bedroom she plopped down on the edge of the unmade bed and gazed unhappily at her opened clothes closet. It was jammed with clothing, none of it organized. Expensive dresses that should have been on hangers lay crumpled on the floor. The shoe rack that hung on the closet door was overstuffed with shoes. As she scanned the room, she saw her reflection in the vanity dresser mirror and groaned miserably. Her complexion was blotchy and she was getting a double chin. *When did I get to be forty years old,* she thought.

On the bedside stand the digital clock switched to 8:50. She rose up from the bed and pulled her neon pink terry cloth bathrobe tight around her body and walked to the kitchen.

The dirty breakfast dishes were on the table and the aroma of fried eggs and bacon hung in the air. She put the silverware and plates in the sink, then sat down at the table and nibbled on a piece of dry and slightly burnt toast. When there was a knock on the kitchen door she got up with the toast still held in her teeth. She opened the door.

The toast fell from her mouth, dropping onto one of her slippers.

Holding two bags of groceries and standing in front of her, the young man said, "Good morning, Mrs. Fields, I have your order." His smile was an orthodontist's dream.

"Who are you?" she stammered.

"I'm Brent. I'll be delivering your groceries from now on. Doug got a new job," he said.

"How old are you?" she said as she stared at his cleft chin, thick pink lips, perfectly shaped Roman nose and startling, crystal blue eyes. His skin was so smooth and unblemished that she had to stuff her hands in the bathrobe pockets to keep from running her hand across his face. She wanted to run her fingers through his thick, black wavy hair.

"I just turned twenty-one," he said. "Where would you like me to put the bags?"

"On the table," she said.

As he placed them on the table, she stared at him, mouth agape. His biceps bulged in his short-sleeved shirt and the muscles in his back made the shirt ripple. As he turned around she averted her eyes to keep from looking at his crotch.

She grabbed her change purse from the shelf by the door and took out a twenty-dollar bill and handed it to him. "Thank you so much for delivering my groceries."

"Wow, this is very generous," he said, looking at the money. "I'll be back next week with your next order."

"I hope so," she said.

He went out the door. She rested against it, breathless and feeling feverish.

*

On his way out the door, George kissed Claire lightly on the cheek.

Her entire body tingled with anticipation. Thoughts that Brent would soon be delivering the groceries made her cheeks burn with excitement. She had it all worked out how she was going to seduce him. The nights of lying awake at night and imagining being in his arms, receiving his kisses and feeling his naked body on hers had fueled her desire to the brink of sexual frenzy. To his delight, her husband was treated as a sex toy the entire week, but it was Brent she was thinking about.

Hurriedly she straightened up the living room, then rushed into the bedroom and made the bed and closed the closet door. She kicked off her slippers and removed all of her clothes and tossed them into the clothes hamper. In the closet she found a leather mini skirt and a blouse with a plunging neckline and a pair of black spiked heels. She decided not to wear a bra or panties. Before she dressed she doused herself with perfume. At the vanity mirror she brushed her hair so that it looked fuller and put makeup on. Before leaving the bedroom she stood in front of the mirror and felt certain he wouldn't be able to resist her despite their age differences.

In the kitchen she quickly cleared the table of the breakfast dishes. She looked at the clock above the refrigerator. It was 9:30, the scheduled time for the delivery. She sat in a chair and nervously chewed on her lower lip as she waited.

The knock on the door made her jump. She leapt up from the chair and opened the door.

"Good morning, Mrs. Fields," Brent said.

She pulled him into the house, closed the door, and grabbed the bags and put them on the table. Then she threw herself into his arms. "Take me, Brent," she said as she smothered his neck with kisses.

He pushed her back and held her at arm's length. "Please stop, Mrs. Fields. I'm gay."

It was like being punched in the gut. She dropped back in a chair, exhausted and humiliated. "Take five dollars from my change purse and I'll see you next week," she said.

Let Our Resting Places Burn Like Roman Candles

Joseph S. Pete

The first time they set the bed on fire, it was skittering back—motored by their shimmying motion—toward the closet, over some strewn-about candles she asked him to light to set the mood.

"Saints alive!" he blurted out as flames flashed high, not really knowing from whence that exclamation came.

He slid free, grabbed the burning blanket and beat it on the floor until the last, fading embers died. He dashed to the kitchen, frantically cast about for a pot or a vase, ended up snatching an orange juice carton and doused the charred fabric with the thick, pulpy juice. For good measure, he started stomping on the damp, burnt blanket with his bare foot.

"Honey, it's okay."

"Dear, you can't be too careful," he insisted. "One little lingering cinder can reignite a fire. A huge blaze could snuff us out while we sleep. The smoke, that's what gets you. They always die of smoke inhalation during those house fires. They get trapped, and succumb to the smoke."

The ruined blanket got pitched. All the candles went into hibernation in the hall closet.

They made light of it. She recounted a story her friend had told her about an old drunk the fire department rescued from a burning bed. A firefighter chastised him for falling asleep with a lit cigarette and he countered with, "listen smart guy, the bed was on fire when I went to sleep."

But he was troubled by the experience. He started to send her articles about unfortunate souls who were burned beyond recognition or completely incinerated by bed fires caused by careless smoking or overheated smartphones. He'd tell her about how people ended up marooned in burn wards for months, and how severe burns was supposed to be one of the most painful injuries to recover from.

"Dear, it's okay," she'd say before goofily breaking into a half-remembered rendition of Billy Joel's *We Didn't Start the Fire*.

She segued to The Righteous Brothers: *We've Got That Burning Feeling*.

"Isn't it *We've Lost That Loving Feeling*?" he asked. "So shouldn't it be *We've Lost That Burning Feeling*? Which wouldn't make sense. Or wait, actually it would perfectly describe…"

"Whatever." She rolled her eyes, stormed into the kitchen and heated a cup of tea in the microwave.

The second time they set the bed on fire, the reintroduced candles were again the culprits. They drifted off into the arms of Morpheus in their joint embrace with the wicks still lit. One somehow toppled off the dresser later that night.

She smelled something, and awoke to a wall of leaping fire. It was startling but looked more dramatic than it was, and they quickly extinguished the flames again.

Nostrils thick with a smoky stench, he soon had every last candle in the apartment rounded up and cinched in a trash bag. He even tossed the oatmeal cookie-scented candle he bought from a hip boutique for her birthday, the one she only occasionally uncorked and sniffed for comfort but never lit.

That was it. He decided they couldn't risk candles, matches, the grill lighter, anything that could end in their inadvertent funeral pyre.

He hauled the hefty plastic bag that hung slack over his shoulder across the rain-slicked pavement of the parking lot of their apartment complex, under the moon's faint luminescence and the flickering of a forlorn streetlamp.

Self-awareness coursed over him. The moment felt freighted, fateful.

"Hell," he thought as he stood before the dumpster, candle-stuffed bag in hand. "I hope to hell this doesn't symbolize a thing. Let this be literal. Please God, let this be literal."

Patience

Andrea Diede

I breathe in the smell of beached seaweed that creeps in through the loft's only window and listen for the massive gong of the clock tower.

Rays of light dance through the window forming triangles on the oak floor. I grasp the fruit from the side table in my palm. I admire the contrast between my powder white skin and the golden apple.

The clock tower sounds, my first appointment is arriving soon. I return the apple and rise from my chair. The scent of the ocean mingles with the roses sitting on the vanity next to the door.

The doorbell chimes and my stomach flutters. I remove the silk shawl from my shoulders and drape it over my chair. The doorbell rings for the second time. I peek into the mirror of the vanity, run my fingertips along my eyebrows and pinch my cheeks. A herculean knock echoes through the loft. "Patience." I smear a tinted gloss over my pursed lips.

I stand in front of the door, pushing my right hip out to accentuate its curve. I open the door, and there stands a burly gentleman, fiddling with his keys. I inhale, pulling up ribs inward to draw the man's gaze to my cleavage.

"You're late for your session." I twirl around, and he follows me inside.

"Please." I glide my hand along the back of the chaise lounge, fingers following the embroidered thread. "Sit." He hurries to sit.

"How was your week?" I retreat to my chair across from him. His eyes follow every contour of my body, every fold, every feminine swell.

"It was," he gawks at the lace trim accentuating my bosoms, "fair."

"Fair?" I twine my finger around the chain of my necklace. "And what about your date?"

"I slept with her." He leans towards me, elbows on knees.

"Why?"

"I suppose," he stutters, "to make you jealous."

"Why would that make me jealous?" I lean towards him with my elbows on my knees, reflecting his positioning. "Ares, we have discussed this before." I stand and slide one heel in front of the other until I am standing in front of him. "I am your therapist, nothing more." The color drains from his face.

"I thought —"

"Shhh." I lean forward putting his face inches from my cleavage. His panting moistens the skin of my breasts. I cradle his face with my thumbs and stretch my long fingers into his hair. He sits taller, yearning for my glossed lips to press against his dry ones. I give in.

I move away when he parts my mouth with his tongue. I whisper in his ear, "Session over." With a jerk, I twist his head, snapping his neck.

His limp body slides down my soft, lean legs as I step backward. I smooth my skirt against my body and return to my chair. I pick up the golden apple and examine its beauty in the light. I pull it into my mouth, and my teeth break into its skin and the sweet nectar dribbles down my chin.

There is another thump on the door.

"Patience."

Couldn't & Wouldn't

DS Levy

Kathleen said she couldn't. But as he ran his fingers through her long brown hair he suggested that maybe what she really meant was that she *wouldn't*.

They were at a classmate's apartment, in the bathroom. The door was locked. On the other side: thumping loud music, students trashed or getting there. The bathroom was coveted property, its door a thin screen between good times and carnality. Before long someone would come along pounding, demanding to use the head – or hoping to get it.

"I don't get what you mean," she whispered, nibbling on his ear. "They're the same, right?"

Technically, no. True, both statements were negatives, both contractions (he was glad she hadn't used the formal, un-contracted form, which seemed flatly final), both declarations of impossibility.

"'Declarations'?" she said, breathing harder. "Now you've lost me."

And he *had* lost her, but not in that way. She opened her eyes, looked bewildered. Her blue eyes were deep swirling pools, tides churning. She was going to fucking cry. Her lips were pursed, not for kissing, but for a good letting go–trembling like a rabbit's. Good God, he hated that! *Please, don't cry, for Christ's sake!*

Too late. Big fat tears rolled out the corners of her eyes, down her downy cheeks. Now her nose was twitching. It made him nervous. It added pressure. He could feel every inch of his skin. He was on top of her, in her. He felt himself growing small, smaller. Her tears reduced him. *Jesus, not now.* His naked body covered her like a wet blanket. His dick was shrinking and with one slight move he'd be outside, a dangling sack, limp and moist between her legs.

Christ, it wasn't like he'd asked her to *marry* him. And he wasn't asking her to do anything any other girl wouldn't do. They all liked it. Or at least pretended to. And they certainly liked it when he did it to them.

Well, fuck. – Actually, that's where they were headed. *In media coitus.* Then he'd had to open his big fat mouth, which is all he'd wanted from her. *Just this once, would you, please? Baby, just for me?* It wasn't like he was begging. He didn't need to beg. He just wanted her to, *you know, this one time.* For him, his pleasure.

But no, it was all about her. Her and her pleasures. She couldn't, or wouldn't. Now he felt her hand reaching for him. Wanting him, wanting it. "It." He wasn't an "it," by God. Like her, he had wants and needs. She *couldn't.* Oh, really? He was pulling himself off her sweaty adhesive skin. He was rolling away, done. "It" was done. All because she *couldn't.* When what she really meant was that she *wouldn't.*

"I don't understand," she said, touching him on the shoulder, her fingertips warm, firmly wanting. "I just said ..."

Not again, he didn't need to hear it twice. He said, "I got it. You won't." Her felt her gaze penetrate him, but he wouldn't look at her. And it wasn't that he couldn't. He just wouldn't.

A Waste of Shame

Robb T. White

An age before internet porn. A time when the big names of burlesque were Blaze Starr and Tempest Storm, a time when you had one friend in the neighborhood whose dad hid nudist magazines in the garage. As little kids, we laughed at Bettie Page's woolly "fur".

On Sundays after mass, I'd beeline to the local pharmacy and the magazine racks where *Glamor Parade*, *Soldier of Fortune*, *Stag*, *True Detective* and the girlie rags drew me with their siren song of lust. It wasn't easy being calm while my eyes raked the pages and followed every insinuating curve of a pinup's breast outlined through a blouse. In the cheapest of these magazines, blowsy women with pasties covering their nipples looked out with bored faces. The mere act of turning pages enhanced the olfactory pleasure from the aroma of the wood pulp, which scored an invisible path of neurons fired from brain to scrotum. Like lightning, only visible on the return trip up to the clouds, that tingling south of the beltline was an addictive drug, and I had to have those magazines.

I don't recall the first girlie magazine I stole. I do have a single memory of a black-and-white photo of an English burlesque model in a beehive hairdo whose floppy breasts and pancake-sized areolae were barely covered by glittering star pasties. Soon I was stealing and slipping them under my shirt (buttons undone in advance).

I was so remorseful for my stealing that I saved up five dollars, put it in an envelope and wrote the word *Restitution* across the front of it. I remember being surprised I could spell the word. I left the envelope near an untended cash register.

They all wound up in the same hiding spot: wrapped in plastic, tucked inside a hollowed log at the end of the block where my house stood, a rat-infested, falling-down factory, where my cousins and I filmed our war movies with his Super-8 movie camera. I can't recall how many of these were secreted in that log, but I do remember slipping away from my house or leaving my friends to check out the women in solitude. At 13, I knew how disreputable these women were, but it didn't matter. They were my secret goddesses. I had no firm understanding of the mechanics of sex (except for a single accidental discovery of my parents in coitus) at this age of pre-Beatles, lollipop-rock, London mod, and beach party movies. Peer-pressure and sports were competitive driving forces in every boy's life. Ducktail hairstyles were out, except for the hillbilly town males, and the Rolling Stones were on the horizon with 'Satisfaction', a tune that had the Youngstown diocese on alert for the corruption of youth. But the music I listened to at night and we heard everywhere on the beach from one blanket of teen girls or boys coming from transistor radios was exclusively the black Motown sound from Detroit.

I discovered masturbation around that summer or it discovered me. My mother never confronted me about my crusted bed sheets, but she had to know. I was in thrall to it, unable to sleep without getting the white stuff out. I recall a humid summer night still restless after three discharges and sleepless still, so I tried thinking of an old woman in a black ankle-length dress shuffling *tap-tapping* across some space under my withering gaze—until even that despicable image too drew forth another ejaculation. This time, terrified at the excessive salvos, I feared I had damaged that organ permanently: nothing but air pumped out from my drained, abused testicles.

These humiliating acts also had to be reported in the confession to a humorless priest who had arrived to replace our beloved priest, whose alcoholism had finally become too much of an embarrassment for the Monsignor in Youngstown to ignore. He was whisked off in the dead of night, and we were informed of his replacement when the new priest stood at the lectern on Sunday for high mass. His Irish brogue was thick but not as thick as his intolerance for young masturbators who couldn't or wouldn't stop their nightly self-floggings. His scolding in the confessional box sticks with me to this day for its curious analogy, even though it's more apt for an oversexed girl: "If somebody gave you a shiny whistle, would you keep blowing it?" By fourteen, I was convinced of my final hellbound destination.

My first stroke book purchase at sixteen is still scored in the channels of my brain somewhere: a shy young beauty is seduced by a worldly older lesbian and later makes her debut before a bevy of pretty lesbians in a pair of red high heels and nothing else. The words are long gone, but I see that scene across a vantage of six decades with no mental exertion.

The first time I legally walked into a porn shop, I felt faint. The glossy cornucopia of bare-it-all flesh was so overwhelming my eyes boxed the room, unable to focus on just one item— and not just the sexy poses of the women gracing the covers but their voluptuous lushness, their inviting smiles from magazine, video carton, or paperback cover, all youth and beauty on display in one room while a prudish town went about its mundane business. My aged slags of the pulps had been replaced by hosts of gorgeous angels.

Today, my jaundiced eye and advanced age recollect those once-risqué articles in the lurid magazines of my youth. Would anyone take seriously articles like 'More and More Women Are Moving into Men's Pads' or 'What Kind of Man Wild Girls Dig the Most'? Facebook, Twitter, YouTube (or, if you prefer, YouPorn), Snapchat *et alia* are this generation's pornography. In the current societal tumult over sexual harassment by Neanderthal men, Shakespeare's coda to Lust in Sonnet 129 carries one timeless message about male humanity's most underrated Deadly Sin: "Savage, extreme, rude, cruel, not to trust."

The Return of Red Ledbetter

Episode 1: The Apartment Upstairs

JP Lundstrom

The dead man lay in the alley, face down in gravel. He hadn't been there long—he wasn't cold yet. Thick, sticky snowflakes floated down, melting as they landed on the man's warmth, keeping everything wet.

Detective Red Ledbetter and his partner, Leo Wilson, walked the scene, flashlight beams thrusting into the night. Fire escapes zigzagged to the tops of buildings. Lights shone in some windows, but no faces appeared.

The stiff wore a tailored suit. Cufflinks, too—and they looked expensive. Well-groomed and well-dressed, he looked out of place in this neighborhood.

Ledbetter pulled a packet from an inside pocket, shook it, and three cigarettes popped up. Grasping one between his lips, he withdrew it, returned the pack to his pocket and lit up. Inhaling gratefully, he stood with his partner to see the body turned over. Together, they studied the handsome face.

"What do you know—a pretty boy." Wilson snorted. "How did this fool manage to get himself killed on Christmas Eve?"

One of the uniforms held out an envelope. "No identification—just this."

Wilson took it, read the address, then snickered. "Peter Dick."

Ledbetter's lip lifted in what might have been a smile, or a sneer.

"Addressed to this building—apartment 810." Wilson nodded toward the building. "You make the call. I'll finish up here."

Ledbetter took a last drag off his smoke then tossed it down, where it fizzled in the snow. Turning away, he left the dead man behind.

He pulled open the glass door and stepped into the building's lobby. Hot, stale air blasted his face, melting the snow on his hat and shoulders. Moisture and odor rose from his heavy wool overcoat.

On the eighth floor, he paused in front of number 812. He never liked delivering bad news.

The door flew open at his knock, and Ledbetter winced. The heat intensified—the woman was a knockout.

Her luminous eyes held him captive. "Who the hell are you?"

A surge of electricity shot through Ledbetter. He touched the rim of his hat, then took it off. "Mrs. Peter Dick?"

Her soft, husky voice caressed his hearing. "Who wants to know?"

His hands tightened, crumpling the hat's brim. "Detective Ledbetter, ma'am."

Silent, she eyed Ledbetter up and down.

"I'll ask again, ma'am. Are you Mrs. Dick?"

"Sure." She leaned against the door, thrusting a hip at him. "You got the letter?"

"You mean this letter?" He tried to think of something—anything—to still his body's response.

"That's the one. Come on in." Ledbetter entered, she stepped towards him, and a luscious tropical scent surrounded them. "What do you want with Pete?"

162

He cleared his throat, shuffled his feet, then clapped his hat back on. "Mr. Dick's body was discovered in the alley about an hour ago."

"Which body was that?" The woman's tongue moistened her full, red lips, and his eyes followed.

"What?" He was confused.

She fondled Ledbetter's tie, and he longed for a taste of her. He put on a grave face and continued. "A man is dead in that alley. A letter in his pocket was addressed to Peter Dick at this apartment. Are you, or are you not, Mrs. Peter Dick?"

"Nah. You'll find that bag of bones in Manor Oaks. She wouldn't be caught dead in this neighborhood."

Ledbetter tried again. "Well then—who are you?"

She almost whispered. "My name is Luz Apagada. It's spelled L-u-z, but you pronounce it 'loose'."

Visions sprang to mind of himself and this woman engaged in loose behavior. He wiped his sweaty hands in his pockets. "Why did you ask which body we found?"

Luz popped the gum in her mouth. "It's complicated. Care to sit, Detective?"

Knees weak, he leaned against the wall. "I'll stand, thanks."

Luz settled into the davenport, kicking off her shoes. "Here's how it works. They show up, give me their letter, and Mrs. Dick—that's me—I take care of the rest."

Ledbetter cleared his throat again. "So you're saying the name isn't accurate?"

"That's not all I'm saying." The bubble she blew popped on her lips, and Ledbetter held his breath, watching her tongue wipe it away. "I'm saying I haven't a clue what this Dick's real name is."

She wiggled her toes, admiring painted nails that matched her lipstick. "If you want anything else, you'll have to talk to the missus."

He pictured his rough hands on her silky legs. "She lives in Manor Oaks?"

"Isn't that what I said?"

"If you think of anything else," Ledbetter straightened his lean, muscular frame. "Here's my card."

"Are you sure there's nothing else?"

There was something else. He wanted her, to take her in his arms, crush his mouth on hers, feel her naked body against his, plunge himself into her depths. His mind resisted, but his body would not be denied. Unbidden, his feet carried him toward her.

He heard the brittle crash of breaking glass and nothing else. The woman's body jerked, her mouth and eyes open in surprise. She gasped and fell forward into Ledbetter's arms. He thought she might have tried to tell him something, but no sound came from her mouth. Her eyes lost their focus and she sagged against him.

He lowered her body to the floor, hiding from the broken window, but there were no more shots. Then he radioed his partner and sat on the floor beside the dead temptress to wait for the medical examiner's team.

A different group of cops and techs joined him. When they were done with him they turned him loose and he made his way out. In moments, the woman had carried him to the heights of desire, and then he was returned to the depths of his loneliness. He staggered, bumping into someone he barely noticed. "Excuse me."

The elevator car arrived, doors yawning open. He stepped forward, ready to be carried down, away from all this, when he heard a cry.

"Ledbetter, wait!"

164

Ooh La La… How I'm (Slowly) Outgrowing the Inner Predator

Bear Jack Gebhardt

Recently, driving down the street, I spotted a hunched up little old lady, dressed in a heavy overcoat, using a cane, making her way down the walk, pulling a shopping cart.

Ooh la la, I said to myself.

That was my *ooh la la* meditation practice.

My old lady utterance was an attempt to balance out the accidental, spontaneous *ooh la la* that had risen up in me a few blocks earlier. A lovely young blond at a stoplight looked over, saw me watching, smiled then looked away. I suspect I reminded her of her grandfather.

On seeing the blond, *ooh la la*, or non-grandfatherly words, images and energies even more guttural spontaneously rose up in me without my bidding. It happens less and less these days, but it does still happen.

I'm a householder monk, and Senior Librarian at Heart Mountain Monastery. Being ordinary dudes, we monks experience as much of the inner sexual predator as the next guy—maybe more. That's one of the reasons we gravitate toward monk-dom, daily meditators, clumsily working to help

165

evolve the species, particularly the male half. We monks just want to give ourselves, and the ladies around us, a little breathing room. A little decency. *Ooh la la* indeed.

Our Abbot suggested that particular *ooh la la* meditation practice to help us become more aware of our inner predator conditioning. And maybe let some of it go. "We need to be equal opportunity *ooh la la* guys," he suggested. Thus, my *ooh la la* for the little old lady.

In regards to this inner predator conditioning, I'm innocent, as are we all. As we males come into adolescence we are taught to make the *ooh la la* (predator) response when seeing a pretty lady. Sometimes shortened to, *"ooh, ooh"*. We learn it simply by hanging out with older guys on the block and watching how grown men act. *Ooh la la* has been the common ground with other guys since cave men days.

We—or least I—learned the *ooh la la* response even before I had a clear grasp on what *ooh la la* might actually lead to, or even meant. I was conditioned before my inner hormones had awakened. I didn't understand why I should relate to ladies that way.

As I matured, of course, I did learn. My inner hormones did awaken, as did my curiosity. The "other sex" was no longer just a nuisance, like the tattletale girl Mary Alice who lived down the block. The other sex might become a wonderful friend, like Linda Duke next door, or someone to play jacks with, like Robin Norton, another neighbor.

As I moved deeper into adolescence, a delicious mystery arose regarding these ladies. How are they different, and how are they the same as we guys? Obviously, there was—there is— a difference. Not only physically, but also in the way we think and feel and play life games (like the game of being a monk). But we're also the same. How strange, how mysterious, how wonderful and curious this is.

166

But, alas, in contemporary culture, the primary sexual conditioning for adolescent boys might best be summarized by a 2005 book written by Neil Strauss entitled, *The Game— Penetrating the Secret Society of Pickup Artists*. That book details how professional pickup artists, some of whom charge $2500 and up for a weekend seminar, view finding a beautiful woman to have sex with as a game. Secret tricks, tips and strategies can be learned, and shared. The winner of this game is he who has sex with the most women.

For most adolescent guys, that seems like a pretty cool game. *Ooh la la.*

Thankfully, just as we were learning The Game, in response to such misogyny and the culture of the times, came the feminist movement—a widespread, non-hierarchical awakening of the "equal rights" of women. So Robyn and Linda and even Mary Alice started talking to us about the way things were—are—and should be. And Betty Friedan and Gloria Steinem (*"a woman without a man is like a fish without a bicycle"*) and the National Organization of Women gave political, intellectual and historical depth to the need for a change in consciousness, a change in what we were thinking. A change in our *ooh la la* conditioning.

And we also had the war, and Janis Joplin, Joan Baez, Peter Paul and Mary and the Mamas and the Papas—the experience of ladies and men who stood as equals at the barricades, against the violent idiocy of the times.

And then I got married, and had both a son and a daughter who grew up in the 70s and 80s. I had to learn all over again what it meant to be a man, a woman, exposed here in this new millennium not only to the idiocy of the old ways but miraculously the delicious, inescapable goddess energy now flooding—and rebalancing—the planet.

Come to find out, The Game was—and is—selfishly played mostly to impress other men. And it consistently, inevitably, viciously creates lose-lose types of relationships.

The good news was—is—that *ooh la la* does not arise from our deepest self. Our deepest self is already content, at peace, fulfilled and our deepest relationship with other people is based on sharing that peace, that contentment, that inherent joy.

More specifically, when we go beyond our conditioning we discover we are consciousness itself. The biggest surprise, and the deepest intimacy comes in experiencing that single door that opens between two minds. Not a similar door. A *single* door. We are the same consciousness. The same being.

When we move beyond our conditioning, we simply experience each other as differing expressions of this single being. It's a wonderfully penetrating experience which can be shared quietly, harmlessly, anonymously with a stranger on the street, even a little old lady pulling a shopping cart.

Ooh la la, mademoiselle. Pleased to make your acquaintance.

The Recent History of the Sánchez Family Tragedies: Part 1

Guilie Castillo Oriard

In the beginning there was the coveting. Inevitable, perhaps: brother will envy brother, it is the core of human nature. Happens everywhere, in every family.

But not every family's history is this violent.

Tragedy was coded into our DNA a long time ago. And sin. Or, rather, the *accrual* of sin. Sin begetting sin, sin after sin to bury the sins that came before, for a century—maybe more, who knows.

It began, as I said, with the coveting. Or lust, if you prefer. You're all too familiar with the carnal version, despite your vows. (Or because of them.) But there's more to lust than just the satisfaction of the flesh. Perhaps your vows have not protected you from that, either.

Back when her life stretched ahead of her in pristine pages of possibility, and long before she ever imagined being anyone's 'Nana', even anyone's mother, she was known only as Maura Haley. Her father fled starvation in England to forge a life in the New World by his wits (and by the color of his skin; in this land of perennially belittled brown skin, blond hair and green eyes open more doors than any diploma). A Purépecha mother who spoke little Spanish and zero English when the Brit of green eyes absconded with her from a railroad outpost in Michoacán and brought her to the capital (willing or otherwise, we'll never know; details of that drama are lost to us now). Seven older brothers and five older sisters, all but one promptly married off. Elena, the youngest, had inherited spinsterhood: hers by birth and by tradition was the responsibility of caring for her parents until their death.

And then Maura came along. The thirteenth child. Imagine Elena's relief, only nine but fully aware of her destiny, at the passing of her cup of bondage to another. But Papa took a fancy to the newborn, to the green eyes that were his own, to the lock of hair exactly the chestnut of his favorite sister's, Maureen, after whom he insisted this surprise child be named. Mother, too, perhaps due to the difficult pregnancy, developed a special affection for the baby. Perhaps, after twelve children, neither parent had much energy left for discipline. So Elena was released, yes, but then subjected to years of Maura spoiled to what must have seemed, in light of how everyone else was raised, extravagant lengths.

Maybe Elena was right. Maybe Maura, less indulged, would have accepted her fate. Maybe indulgence was the original sin.

Or maybe Maura did accept. Maybe everything that happened truly was an accident, a misstep without forethought.

When Maura graduated, at sixteen, with a secretarial diploma, Papa astonished everyone (maybe even himself) by letting her take a job nearby, an import-export franchise owned by a German expatriate, well-known in the community, a pillar of culture and industriousness. What was the harm, he argued to his wife when she protested; they were both still perfectly healthy, in no need of any special care yet. And the girl hadn't ever given them a single sleepless night, had she?

The German had a son, seventeen, who was being groomed to take his father's place when the time came. Maura kept no photographs of him; perhaps she never had any. It all happened so fast. We don't even know his name. The one thing about him we do know is that he had eyes of a blue so clear they put the summer sky to shame. We know this because no one in the Haley clan ever had eyes like that. It's his eyes you see, as your father and your grandfather did before you, every time you look in the mirror.

Did she lust for him, or he for her? Perhaps it was mutual? Was it a dalliance for him, a wild oat sown before the rigor of respectability set in? And, for her, was it defiance, a gauntlet thrown at Papa's feet? Or was it surrender, a swimmer tired of fighting the current who gives in to exhaustion even as the knowledge crystallizes: *So this is what death feels like?*

It boils down to this: was it lust, or was it love? Are they mutually exclusive? Left to their own devices, could these two child-adults, the blue-eyed and the green-eyed, have had a lifetime not just of passion but of real, honest-to-Christ *love?* Would our family have found redemption, perhaps bypassed condemnation altogether, if Elena's eyes—not her father's green but her mother's brown—hadn't been so sharp, even at dusk, and hadn't picked out, then recognized not just the two silhouettes profiled in the Ford Phaeton's back window but the implications of the way they moved together, merging in the darkness, *into* the darkness, sensuous and primeval and completely out of place in the midst of concrete and civilization?

What did she say, as she barged into the family kitchen? Did she scream accusations? Profess indignation at the sullying of her family's name? Perhaps she exulted in triumph—

haughty, perfect Maura receiving her just desserts at *her* hand, o divine retribution!—or raged at being married to an insipid man incapable of even a tenth of the passion she'd just witnessed.

Who knows what state of undress they were in when Papa dragged them out of the car. What he said, or did, to the boy. What he said, or did, to his daughter. We know this: Maura, my Nana, never saw her lover again. War was brewing in Europe; perhaps his father shipped him off to the *Vaterland* to fulfill the family's patriotic duty. Or to Canada, to continue his education. Or Asia, or Africa, or South America. The world was much larger back then. In any case, he vanished from Maura's world without a trace.

Until the baby came. The baby of the blue, blue eyes who would, one day, kill his brother.

The Butcher's Wife

Nan Wigington

She wrote when she thought he wasn't looking. Notes about the business. On the brown paper she wrapped the bloody bits in, little red blotches swelling beneath black letters. He believed she had taken an interest in the business and this was her way of loving him and remembering butchery. He wasn't sorry that he had married a younger woman. She was strong, could carry on.

Once he saw her write, "The carcass can be chilled or hot boned."

Another time – "Secondary butchering is the trimming of primal cuts."

At night, after flank steaks and potatoes in their little apartment above the little shop, she would serve him tea and he would try to tell her all his secrets.

"Every carcass is different," he would say, "You want to see muscle on the bone. The color of the fat, too, is important. Yellow means grass fed. White is grain."

But the old butcher got too sleepy too soon. His lessons were short, lacked purpose and passion. Barely five sentences and he would rise, peck his wife on the cheek, and go to bed. He worried that he'd never tell her enough. Sometimes he had nightmares. How she might botch a job, cut off his hand, wrap it in brown paper. Sometimes he saw suet with his kidney still attached. One night he thought he woke up to laughter from the other room – hers and another man's. They seemed excited by the carnage.

"Just because I want to cut him up doesn't mean I don't love the old animal," she said clearly. But wasn't it just part of the nightmare? She was a good woman. How could he marry someone so secretive and callous?

The next morning, he smiled as she flirted with the customers, one boy in particular, dressed like a rich man's son.

"I can give you whatever you want," she was saying.

He knew she was only drumming up business, selling more meat to a boy who had enough already. The butcher smiled. An odd wave of pride and lust pushed him toward the pair. He held her from behind, feeling her sinew and muscle, and added –

"We can kill the beast and cut it to your specifications."

"I'm sure you can," the young man said as he accepted an additional brown paper package from the butcher's wife.

That night, they both went to bed directly after tea. The butcher tried to make love, but he began to worry about the young man. Had he been a voice in the old man's nightmare? How often had he come to the shop? How many packages had he already received? How many notes had she written to him? Which were about butchery and which were about love? Nothing on the old man seemed to work. He fell away from his wife in a sad, jealous heap. But she wouldn't give up.

She asked, "So how do you kill the beast?" Then licked her lips.

"You take a bolt gun stunner," he said, lifting his right thumb and index finger. "You touch it to a special place –" He aimed low, then touched high – the middle of her forehead right above her eyes. "Then bam. That's it. You hoist him up, bleed him, take off the hide."

"And split him?" she said as she mounted her husband's hips.

174

"Yes," he whispered.

The butcher's wife touched the center of his forehead, touched each of his breasts, and said, "Bam. Bam. Bam." His body felt strong and whole again. The love was so good, the butcher felt as blissful as a beast gone to slaughter.

Send My Baby Home

Michael Webb

I am overheated and cranky. I am dressed for the cold, which means I begin to swelter the second I get inside. I am standing in a line, trying to pay for a small bracelet, a Christmas gift that my niece will probably hate, and I can feel sweat pooling in the small of my back, underneath my long sweater and my thick winter coat. I could take off the coat, but that means having to carry it, and that is as unappealing as continuing to be hot and disgruntled. I don't think this tiny gift will even be noticed, but one of the rules I have learned to follow in my family is that, at all costs, you should try not to be noticed.

The line is moving forward, and I think about my aching feet, and the unpleasant phone calls I will be making when I get back to the office, and the onrushing holiday season with the forced cheer and pseudo bonhomie and how badly I would rather just sleep them all away. Nothing quite like hearing about Sarah's pregnancy and Corrine's promotion and Dustin's business expanding again to reinforce where exactly you fall in the familial pecking order. There are rules about family gatherings, and you learn them quick: deflect, evade, deny, dissemble. Never let them know your heart.

The last time Shea skyped with me, she laughed when I tried to explain that. "That's such bullshit!" she said, the internet connection from Whateveristan making her words wobble. "If they don't love you as you are? Fuck 'em!" I tried to explain that I wasn't like her, that I couldn't just burn things down when they weren't to my liking, but she blew through my explanation like a troublesome enemy roadblock. "You get one life, hun. One. Don't waste it pretending to be who they want." I knew she meant it.

There is a Melissa Etheridge song playing on the store's intercom. The woman in front of me is shifting her weight from hip to hip, letting out little puffs of impatience as she rocks on high-heeled boots. I wonder who she goes home to at night, what obligations bring her to a store in the middle of the day during the Christmas rush. We share this slow moving line, but I know she is going home to a spouse. I know it, I can feel it, and Shea is thousands of miles from me, and I can feel every inch of that distance.

I am struggling to breathe. I'm usually able to keep Shea at arms' length, but she is suddenly in my blood, inside my skin. I want her, but more than wanting a bedmate, I suddenly want her touch, her presence, her nearness in a way that makes me almost pant. I am consumed by need, full of the gap in my soul that she fills. Melissa is asking Santa to bring her baby home, and the only thing in the world that I want more is my next breath of air.

Also from Pure Slush Books

https://pureslush.com/store/

 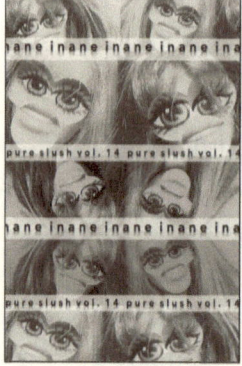 

- Happy² Pure Slush Vol. 15
ISBN: 978-1-925536-39-3 (paperback) / 978-1-925536-40-9 (eBook)
- Inane Pure Slush Vol. 14
ISBN: 978-1-925536-17-1 (paperback) / 978-1-925536-18-8 (eBook)
- Freak Pure Slush Vol. 13
ISBN: 978-1-925536-15-7 (paperback) / 978-1-925536-16-4 (eBook)
- Summer Pure Slush Vol. 12
ISBN: 978-1-925536-13-3 (paperback) / 978-1-925536-14-0 (eBook)
- tall…ish Pure Slush Vol. 11
ISBN: 978-1-925101-80-5 (paperback) / 978-1-925101-98-0 (eBook)
- Five Pure Slush Vol. 10
ISBN: 978-1-925101-71-3 (paperback) / 978-1-925101-72-0 (eBook)

www.ingramcontent.com/pod-product-compliance
Lightning Source LLC
Chambersburg PA
CBHW050739250626
47155CB00005B/1832